LAFAYETTE

D0018267

Shakespeare on the Double!™

Julius Caesar

Shakespeare on the Double!™

Julius Caesar

CONTRA COSTA COUNTY LIBRARY

translated by

Mary Ellen Snodgrass

3 1901 03894 6820

Wiley Publishing, Inc.

Copyright © 2006 by Wiley Publishing, Inc. All rights reserved.

Published by Wiley Publishing, Inc., Hoboken, New Jersey

No part of this publication may be reproduced, stored in a retrieval system or transmitted in any form or by any means, electronic, mechanical, photocopying, recording, scanning or otherwise, except as permitted under Sections 107 or 108 of the 1976 United States Copyright Act, without either the prior written permission of the Publisher, or authorization through payment of the appropriate per-copy fee to the Copyright Clearance Center, 222 Rosewood Drive, Danvers, MA 01923, (978) 750-8400, fax (978) 646-8600, or on the web at www.copyright.com. Requests to the Publisher for permission should be addressed to the Legal Department, Wiley Publishing, Inc., 10475 Crosspoint Blvd., Indianapolis, IN 46256, (317) 572-3447, fax (317) 572-4355, or online at http://www.wiley.com/go/permissions.

Wiley, the Wiley Publishing logo, Howell Book House, and related trademarks are trademarks or registered trademarks of John Wiley & Sons, Inc. and/or its affiliates. All other trademarks are the property of their respective owners. Wiley Publishing, Inc. is not associated with any product or vendor mentioned in this book.

The publisher and the author make no representations or warranties with respect to the accuracy or completeness of the contents of this work and specifically disclaim all warranties, including without limitation warranties of fitness for a particular purpose. No warranty may be created or extended by sales or promotional materials. The advice and strategies contained herein may not be suitable for every situation. This work is sold with the understanding that the publisher is not engaged in rendering legal, accounting, or other professional services. If professional assistance is required, the services of a competent professional person should be sought. Neither the publisher nor the author shall be liable for damages arising here from. The fact that an organization or Website is referred to in this work as a citation and/or a potential source of further information does not mean that the author or the publisher endorses the information the organization or Website may provide or recommendations it may make. Further, readers should be aware that Internet Websites listed in this work may have changed or disappeared between when this work was written and when it is read.

For general information on our other products and services or to obtain technical support please contact our Customer Care Department within the U.S. at (800) 762-2974, outside the U.S. at (317) 572-3993 or fax (317) 572-4002.

Wiley also publishes its books in a variety of electronic formats. Some content that appears in print may not be available in electronic books. For more information about Wiley products, please visit our web site at www.wiley.com.

Library of Congress Cataloging-in-Publication data is available from the publisher upon request.

ISBN-13 978-0-470-04157-4
ISBN-10 0-470-04157-9

Printed in the United States of America

10 9 8 7 6 5 4 3 2 1

Book design by Melissa Auciello-Brogan
Book production by Wiley Publishing, Inc. Composition Services

Contents

Introduction 1

Synopsis 3

List of Characters 11

Character Map 15

Cycle of Death 16

ACT I

Scene 1. 18

Scene 2. 24

Scene 3. 44

ACT II

Scene 1. 56

Scene 2. 76

Scene 3. 84

Scene 4. 86

ACT III

Scene 1. 90

Scene 2. 110

Scene 3. 126

ACT IV

Scene 1. 130

Scene 2. 134

Scene 3. 138

ACT V

    Scene 1. 160

    Scene 2. 168

    Scene 3. 170

    Scene 4. 178

    Scene 5. 182

Questions for Reflection **189**

About the Translator

Mary Ellen Snodgrass is an award-winning author of textbooks and general reference works and a former columnist for the *Charlotte Observer*. A member of Phi Beta Kappa, she graduated magna cum laude from the University of North Carolina at Greensboro and Appalachian State University and holds degrees in English, Latin, psychology, and the education of gifted children.

Introduction

Shakespeare on the Double! Julius Caesar provides the full text of the Bard's play side by side with an easy-to-read modern English translation that you can understand. You no longer have to wonder what exactly "The valiant never taste of death but once" means! You can read the Shakespearean text on the left-hand pages and check the right-hand pages when Shakespeare's language stumps you. Or you can read only the translation, which enables you to understand the action and characters at a more even pace. You can also read both, referring easily between the original text and the modern translation. Any way you choose, you can now fully understand every line of the Bard's masterpiece!

We've also provided you with some additional resources:

- **Brief synopsis** of the basic plot and action provides a broad-strokes overview of the play.
- **Comprehensive character list** covers the actions, motivations, and characteristics of each major player.
- **Visual character map** displays who the major characters are and how they relate to each other.
- **Cycle of death** pinpoints the sequence of deaths in the play, including who dies, how they die, and why they die.
- **Reflective questions** help you delve even more into the themes and meanings of the play.

Reading Shakespeare can be slow and difficult. No more! With *Shakespeare on the Double! Julius Caesar,* you can read the play in language that you can grasp quickly and thoroughly.

Synopsis

ACT I

Scene 1

On the feast of the Lupercal in mid-February, Julius Caesar, a Roman general, receives a victor's parade into Rome. Commoners celebrate his victory over Pompey and his sons in a civil war. Two tribunes, Flavius and Marullus, scold disloyal fans for forgetting their regard for Pompey and for applauding his enemy.

Scene 2

Caesar and his procession enter on their way to a ritual foot race. A fortune teller warns Caesar to beware March 15. Caesar, arrogant and overconfident, dismisses the man as a dreamer and brushes by him. During the foot race, Cassius draws Brutus into conversation outside the arena to discuss Rome's political unrest. Cassius resents and envies Caesar for becoming Rome's absolute dictator. Cassius describes Caesar as the only mortal who dares think of himself as a god.

Brutus does not echo Cassius' envy, but he does worry that too much power to the dictator means less freedom for Romans. Brutus' greatest fear is that fans of Caesar will offer him a crown, thus replacing the republic with a monarchy. The dilemma between loyalty to his friend and respect and patriotism for Rome gnaws at Brutus. Cassius manipulates the inner conflict to persuade Brutus to acknowledge that Rome's survival depends on the assassination of Caesar.

When the procession exits the race, Caesar remarks to his loyal friend Mark Antony that Cassius looks untrustworthy. Lest he seem fearful, Caesar claims to fear no one. When the followers move on, Casca joins Brutus and Cassius and reports that Antony offered Caesar a crown three times. And three times, Caesar pushed the crown aside, each time a little less eagerly. The public spectacle ended with Caesar's collapse from an epileptic seizure. The sickness endeared him to the people. Cicero said something in Greek, but Casca didn't understand him. When Casca and Brutus depart, Cassius reveals that he intends to corrupt Brutus and draw him into a conspiracy against Caesar. The importance of Brutus to the plot derives from his prestige as an honorable Roman of unquestionable morals.

Scene 3

In the street during a thunderstorm, Cicero encounters Casca, who reports on strange omens—fire from heaven, flame burning harmlessly around a slave's hand, and a lion walking by the Capitol. Cicero learns that Caesar will come to the Capitol the next day and hurries out of the storm.

Cassius meets briefly with Casca and instructs him to leave forged letters in Brutus' chair. The messages urge Brutus to take pity on Rome, which Caesar appears to have in a stranglehold. Cassius is determined to bind Casca, Decius Brutus, Caius Ligarius, Cinna, Metellus, and Trebonius in an execution plot.

ACT II

Scene 1

Late at night, Brutus paces restlessly in his orchard and orders his servant Lucius to light a candle in the study. Brutus finds the forged letters from Cassius and ponders the seriousness of Rome's situation. With faces concealed, the conspirators converge at his house to discuss their plan. By now a willing participant, Brutus declares that they must act nobly and without stealth. Cassius insists that they kill Mark Antony as well. Brutus counters Cassius and claims that the group should not think of themselves as butchers but sacrificers.

After the conspirators depart, Portia asks her husband about his recent restlessness and about the late-night meeting. He tries to conceal the plot and claims that he has been ill. A woman of noble ancestry, Portia reminds her husband that she is the daughter of Cato, Rome's censor. In proof of her courage, she reveals a wound that she has inflicted on her thigh to show that she is able to keep a secret. Moved by her act, he promises to tell her what has been troubling him. When Caius Ligarius arrives with a bandage on his head, Brutus urges him to take part in an act that will heal Rome.

Scene 2

After a frightening storm in the night, Calpurnia, Caesar's wife, awakens on March 15. She is shaken by a terrifying dream in which Caesar's statue poured blood that citizens washed in. She pleads with him to remain home from the Senate. Augurers sacrifice an animal and find no heart. They agree that the signs indicate that Caesar should stay home.

At Calpurnia's urging, Caesar decides to forego the Senate session, but Decius Brutus, a friend who secretly works for the conspirators, reinterprets Calpurnia's dream from a positive angle. He describes the bleeding statue as the nurturer of Roman citizens. He persuades Caesar to attend to public duty or else be laughed at for fearing a woman's dreams. Caesar agrees and shares wine with the conspirators before leaving for the day's work.

Scene 3

On the way to the Senate House, Artemidorus, a grammarian, stands in the street. He is ready to hand Caesar a note. The message alerts Caesar to the conspirators' intentions.

Scene 4

Portia, terrified at the plot that her husband is involved in, remains at home. She dispatches the servant boy Lucius for news from the Senate. The boy is confused about what he is supposed to look for. She encounters a fortune teller, who awaits Caesar at a narrow part of the street to warn him of danger. She feels faint as she anticipates news from Lucius and charges females with being weak and unable to keep a secret.

ACT III

Scene 1

As Caesar, his colleagues, and others approach the Capitol, the fortune teller warns that the Ides of March have arrived without incident, but are not yet past. At an opportune moment, Artemidorus stops Caesar and begs that he read a petition. Caesar rejects the personal request until he has completed Senate business. Drawing near the Capitol, the conspirators press around pleading for the return of Metellus Cimber's brother Publius, an exiled citizen.

When Trebonius draws Mark Antony out of the way, the conspirators surround Caesar. After Casca strikes the first blow, the other plotters stab Caesar 33 times. At the advance of Brutus, whom Caesar trusts, Caesar draws his cloak over his face and falls from the final blow. His corpse lies at the base of Pompey's statue. The conspirators bathe their hands and weapons in Caesar's blood.

Immediately, disorder threatens the conspirators' plans. To ingratiate himself with assassins, Mark Antony sends a servant. Assured that he may approach without fear of attack, Mark Antony pretends to concur with the killers' claims that Caesar was a tyrant. Mark Antony seeks Brutus's permission to speak at Caesar's public funeral. Against Cassius' advice, Brutus grants the request. When the conspirators scatter, Antony reveals his fury at the murderers and his intent to transform a moving funeral oratory into the beginning of a bloody civil war. He warns Octavius' servant to keep his master safe from public rage until it is safe to enter the city.

Scene 2

At the public lectern, Brutus sends Cassius to another venue to address the people. Brutus confronts a suspicious crowd. He outlines the reasons that Cassius and the other plotters assassinated Caesar before he gained more power. The people applaud Brutus's noble purpose in halting tyranny and in restoring Roman freedoms. He leaves the pulpit to Mark Antony, whom the crowd suspects of maligning Brutus. At first, Mark Antony appears to yield to the "honorable" plotters and halts to regain control of his sorrow. He soon turns his repeated praise of Brutus and the conspirators into grim sarcasm.

Through skilled rebuttal of Brutus' claims, Mark Antony twists the mob's emotions. He uncovers the bloody corpse and names the assassins who stabbed through Caesar's cloak. At the mob's demand, Mark Antony reads Caesar's will, which gives Rome's citizens cash as well as land for recreational purposes. By the end of Antony's harangue, the populace perceives Brutus and Cassius as brutal killers. The people howl for revenge. Plebeians pour into the thoroughfares, determined to tear the conspirators apart and burn their houses. Brutus, Cassius, and the other plotters flee through the gates. Octavius, Caesar's nephew and only heir, arrives in Rome after receiving a summons earlier from Caesar.

Scene 3

The raving mob happens on Cinna the poet and, thinking him to be Cinna the conspirator, lay hold on him to tear him apart.

ACT IV

Scene 1

At Mark Antony's house, Octavius allies with him. The two join Lepidus in a triumvirate and plot the deaths of the assassins. They agree that all eight and their families must die. Mark Antony reveals that there are rewards awaiting their swift action. Octavius justifies the role of Lepidus as errand boy. Antony and Octavius realize that they must raise an army.

Scene 2

Near Sardis in Turkey, Brutus is camped with his army. He suspects that Cassius is no longer a close friend and ally. When Cassius arrives, he accuses Brutus of maligning him. The two leaders quarrel in view of the soldiers.

Scene 3

In the privacy of the tent, Cassius complains that Brutus has accused Lucius Pella of taking bribes. Brutus accuses Cassius of fiscal corruption and of withholding pay to Brutus' forces. Brutus reminds Cassius that the conspirators killed Caesar as a means of restoring justice to Rome. Cassius retorts that he has more experience and is an abler soldier and leader. Brutus promises to laugh at Cassius for his rages. The two men cool off and shake hands. Brutus rationalizes his anger as a result of the recent death of Portia. She grew depressed during Brutus' absence. As the forces of Mark Antony and Octavius gained strength, she despaired and swallowed live coals.

After Titinius and Messala join Brutus and Cassius for a conference, the two leaders discuss the recent execution of 100 senators, including Cicero. Meanwhile, Antony and Octavius camp at Philippi in southern Macedonia. Cassius prefers to wait for the armies of Antony and Octavius to attack at Sardis, but Brutus opts to assault the position at Philippi. Cassius and Brutus part friends. That night, Brutus listens to his servant Lucius sing while Brutus reads. Caesar's ghost appears to Brutus and promises to see him again at Philippi. Brutus questions Lucius and his guards, Marullus and Flavius, but no one else heard the ghost.

ACT V

Scene 1

Before war breaks out at Philippi, Octavius is delighted that Brutus and Cassius are abandoning the high country at Sardis to attack in Macedonia. The leaders of the two sides trade insults. Mark Antony accuses the conspirators of gross disloyalty to Caesar. Cassius believes that he will soon die. Brutus declares that he will never be displayed as a prisoner of war.

Scene 2

Brutus dispatches Messala across the battlefield with letters for the legions on the opposite hill. The message urges them to sweep down on the plain and overwhelm their enemy.

Scene 3

When Brutus' soldiers obey the command, they succeed and break ranks to loot their enemy. Cassius misinterprets the turmoil on the plain below. Pindarus reports that Mark Antony has seized Cassius' tents. Fearing that the messenger Titinius has fallen to the enemy, Cassius promises freedom to Pindarus if Pindarus will help Cassius commit suicide. Cassius collapses on the sword with which he stabbed Caesar. Messala returns with good news, but finds Cassius dead. Titinius awards the corpse a victory wreath. Titinius then kills himself. Brutus comes upon Cassius' body and promises to grieve for his comrade when he finds time. Brutus leads his soldiers back to battle.

Scene 4

Lucilius lures the enemy away from Brutus by pretending to be Brutus. To instill courage in the troops, young Cato rushes brashly into the fray and dies in combat. After Mark Antony's troops capture Lucilius, Mark Antony realizes that Lucilius has tricked them. Mark Antony orders his men to honor Lucilius for his courage. Men depart to locate and capture Brutus and Octavius. Mark Antony awaits in Octavius' tent.

Scene 5

In the last assault, Brutus' troops flee from defeat. He asks his comrades Dardanius, Clitus, and Volumnius to help him commit suicide, but they refuse. With the aid of Strato, Brutus falls on his sword. He dies claiming to the ghost that he killed himself far more willingly than he stabbed Caesar. Mark Antony and Octavius find Brutus' remains. Octavius promises employment to Brutus' servants, including Strato. Mark Antony praises Brutus as the noblest and least blameworthy of the assassins. All the others envied Caesar, but Brutus acted out of fear for Rome's safety and survival. Octavius orders that Brutus' body lie in state in Octavius's tent.

List of Characters

FLAVIUS AND MARULLUS   Tribunes who wish to protect the plebeians from Caesar's tyranny; they break up a crowd of commoners waiting to witness Caesar's triumph and are "put to silence" during the feast of Lupercal for removing ornaments from Caesar's statues.

JULIUS CAESAR   A successful military leader who wants the crown of Rome. Unfortunately, he has become imperious, easily flattered, and overly ambitious. Eight conspirators assassinate him midway through the play; later, his spirit appears to Brutus at Sardis and also at Philippi.

CASCA   A witness to Caesar's attempts to manipulate the people of Rome into offering him the crown, he reports the failure to Brutus and Cassius. He joins the conspiracy the night before the assassination and is the first conspirator to stab Caesar.

CALPURNIA   The wife of Julius Caesar; she urges him to stay at home on the day of the assassination because of the unnatural events of the previous night as well her prophetic dream in which Caesar's body spurts blood.

MARCUS ANTONIUS (MARK ANTONY)   He appears first as a confidant and a devoted follower of Caesar, and he offers Caesar a crown during the feast of Lupercal. He has a reputation for sensuous living, but he is also militarily accomplished, politically shrewd, and skilled at oratory. He is able to dupe Brutus into allowing him to speak at Caesar's funeral. By his funeral oration, Antony excites the crowd to rebellion. He forms a triumvirate with Lepidus and Octavius. Antony and Octavius defeat Brutus and Cassius at Philippi.

A SOOTHSAYER   He warns Caesar during the celebration of the feast of Lupercal to "beware the ides of March." Only minutes before the assassination, he again warns Caesar as he enters the Senate House.

MARCUS BRUTUS A *praetor;* or judicial magistrate of Rome. He is widely admired for his character and noble family. He joins the conspiracy because he fears that Caesar will become a tyrant. Idealism causes Brutus to make several poor judgments and impedes his ability to understand those who are less honorable than he. Brutus defeats Octavius' forces in the first battle at Philippi, but loses the second battle and commits suicide rather than be taken prisoner.

CASSIUS The brother-in-law of Brutus and an acute judge of human nature, Cassius organizes the conspiracy against Caesar. He recruits Brutus by passionate argument and by dispatching, forged letters to Brutus' office. Cassius argues that Antony should be assassinated along with Caesar, and that Antony should not speak at Caesar's funeral. Cassius lets Brutus convince him to fight Antony and Octavius at Philippi rather than to await the enemy at Sardis. Antony defeats Cassius at the first battle of Philippi. Cassius commits suicide when he mistakenly believes that Antony and Octavius have defeated Brutus.

CICERO A senator and a scholarly orator of Rome. He is calm and philosophical when he meets the excited Casca during the night of portentous tumult preceding the day of the assassination. The triumvirs have him put to death.

CINNA The conspirator who urges Cassius to bring "noble" Brutus into the conspiracy. Cinna assists by placing some of Cassius' forged letters where Brutus will discover them.

LUCIUS Brutus' young servant. Lucius sings for his master in Sardis. Brutus treats him with understanding, gentleness, and tolerance.

DECIUS BRUTUS The conspirator who persuades Caesar to attend the Senate on the day of the ides of March by fabricating a positive interpretation of Calpurnia's portentous dream and by telling Caesar that the Senate intends to crown him king.

METELLUS CIMBER The conspirator who attracts Caesar's attention by requesting that Caesar recall Publius, Metellus's brother, from exile. The distraction allows the assassins to surround Caesar and give Casca the opportunity to stab Caesar from behind.

TREBONIUS A conspirator who concurs with Brutus' argument that Antony be spared. Trebonius lures Antony out of the Senate House so that the other conspirators can kill Caesar without having to fear Antony's intervention. Consequently, Trebonius is the only conspirator who does not actually stab Caesar or see him die.

PORTIA   The wife of Brutus and the daughter of Marcus Cato. She argues that family relationships make her strong enough to conceal Brutus' secrets. On the morning of the assassination, she is extremely agitated by the fear that she will reveal what Brutus has confided to her. She commits suicide when she realizes that Octavius and Antony are gaining in popularity.

CAIUS LIGARIUS   A conspirator who is too ill to attend the meeting at Brutus' house. Although Caius Ligarius does not stab Caesar, irate citizens mark his house for destruction.

PUBLIUS   Clears the way for Caesar on the way to the Capitol. He is stunned as he witnesses the assassination. Brutus sends him out to tell the citizens that the conspirators will not harm them.

ARTEMIDORUS   A supporter of Caesar. Artemidorus gives Caesar a letter at the Capitol. In the letter, he lists the conspirators by name and indicates that they intend an assassination. Caesar does not read the letter.

POPILIUS LENA   The senator who wishes Cassius well in his "enterprise" as Caesar enters the Senate House. This comment intensifies the dramatic tension prior to the assassination by causing Cassius and Brutus to suspect that others know of the plot to murder Caesar.

CINNA THE POET   On his way to attend Caesar's funeral, he encounters rioters stirred by Antony's funeral oration. The mob at first confuses him with Cinna the conspirator, but even after they discover their error, they seize the poet "for his bad verses."

OCTAVIUS CAESAR   The nephew, adopted son, and heir of Julius Caesar. Octavius joins Antony and Lepidus to rule following the death of Caesar. He and Antony lead the army that defeats Cassius and Brutus at Philippi. Octavius honors Brutus' high ideals.

M. AEMILIUS LEPIDUS   A Roman noble who joins Antony and Octavius to form the Second Triumvirate to rule the Roman Empire following the assassination of Caesar. Lepidus is weak. Antony uses him essentially to run errands.

LUCILIUS   The officer who impersonates Brutus at the second battle of Philippi. After his capture, Antony admires his loyalty to Brutus and protects him, hoping that Lucilius will choose to serve him as loyally as he did Brutus.

PINDARUS   A Parthian captive. At Philippi, he erroneously tells his master, Cassius, that Antony has captured the scout Titinius. Actually Brutus' forces celebrate victory with Titinius. Thinking that all is lost, Cassius decides to die. Pindarus stabs him with the same sword that stabbed Caesar.

TITINIUS   An officer in the army of Cassius and Brutus. Titinius guards the tent at Sardis during the argument between the two generals, and takes notes of the army's needs. Titinius guards Cassius at Philippi during a parlay with Antony and Octavius and reports on the outcome of combat. After Cassius commits suicide when he mistakenly believes Titinius to have been taken prisoner by the enemy, Titinius kills himself in emulation of Cassius.

MESSALA   A soldier serving under Brutus and Cassius, Messala gives information concerning the advance of the triumvirs, and he reports Portia's death to Brutus at Sardis. At Philippi, he tries to lift Cassius' spirits and hears Cassius confess that he believes in omens. Messala delivers a message to troops across the battlefield. Later, he discovers Cassius' body and becomes a captive of Antony and Octavius.

VARRO AND CLAUDIUS   Servants of Brutus, they spend the night in his tent at Sardis. Neither of them observes the ghost of Caesar that appears to Brutus.

YOUNG CATO   The son of Marcus Cato, the brother of Portia, the brother-in-law of Brutus, and a soldier in the army commanded by Brutus and Cassius. He dies during the second battle at Philippi while trying to inspire the army by loudly proclaiming that he is the son of Marcus Cato and that he is still fighting.

CLITUS AND DARDANIUS   Servants of Brutus, they refuse their master's request at Philippi to kill him.

VOLUMNIUS   A schoolmate of Brutus and a soldier under his command at Philippi. He refuses to hold a sword for Brutus to impale himself on.

STRATO   The loyal servant who holds Brutus' sword so that he may commit suicide. Later, upon Messala's recommendation, Strato becomes a servant to Octavius.

Character Map

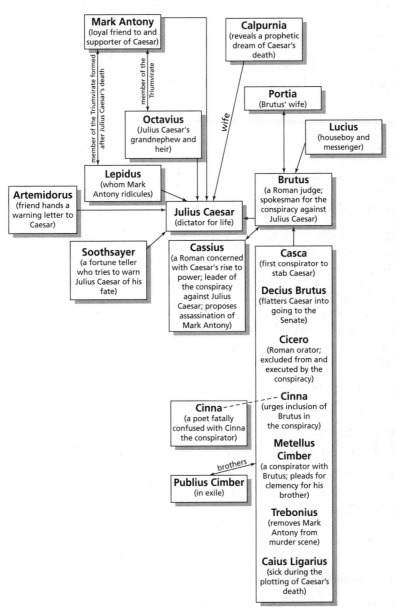

Mark Antony
(loyal friend to and supporter of Caesar)

Calpurnia
(reveals a prophetic dream of Caesar's death)

member of the Triumvirate formed after Julius Caesar's death

member of the Triumvirate

Octavius
(Julius Caesar's grandnephew and heir)

Portia
(Brutus' wife)

wife

Lucius
(houseboy and messenger)

Lepidus
(whom Mark Antony ridicules)

Artemidorus
(friend hands a warning letter to Caesar)

Julius Caesar
(dictator for life)

Brutus
(a Roman judge; spokesman for the conspiracy against Julius Caesar)

Soothsayer
(a fortune teller who tries to warn Julius Caesar of his fate)

Cassius
(a Roman concerned with Caesar's rise to power; leader of the conspiracy against Julius Caesar; proposes assassination of Mark Antony)

Casca
(first conspirator to stab Caesar)

Decius Brutus
(flatters Caesar into going to the Senate)

Cicero
(Roman orator; excluded from and executed by the conspiracy)

Cinna
(urges inclusion of Brutus in the conspiracy)

Cinna
(a poet fatally confused with Cinna the conspirator)

Metellus Cimber
(a conspirator with Brutus; pleads for clemency for his brother)

brothers

Publius Cimber
(in exile)

Trebonius
(removes Mark Antony from murder scene)

Caius Ligarius
(sick during the plotting of Caesar's death)

15

Cycle of Death

Julius Caesar's assassination at the hands of the conspirators begins a cycle of suicide, murder, and death in the play. This death spiral continues until Brutus, one of the lead conspirators, kills himself at the play's end. The graphic below outlines the sequence of deaths that spur the execution plot.

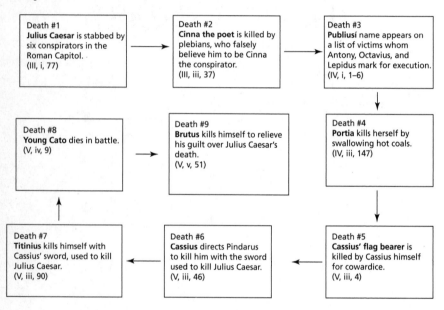

Death #1
Julius Caesar is stabbed by six conspirators in the Roman Capitol.
(III, i, 77)

Death #2
Cinna the poet is killed by plebians, who falsely believe him to be Cinna the conspirator.
(III, iii, 37)

Death #3
Publiusí name appears on a list of victims whom Antony, Octavius, and Lepidus mark for execution.
(IV, i, 1–6)

Death #8
Young Cato dies in battle.
(V, iv, 9)

Death #9
Brutus kills himself to relieve his guilt over Julius Caesar's death.
(V, v, 51)

Death #4
Portia kills herself by swallowing hot coals.
(IV, iii, 147)

Death #7
Titinius kills himself with Cassius' sword, used to kill Julius Caesar.
(V, iii, 90)

Death #6
Cassius directs Pindarus to kill him with the sword used to kill Julius Caesar.
(V, iii, 46)

Death #5
Cassius' flag bearer is killed by Cassius himself for cowardice.
(V, iii, 4)

Shakespeare's
Julius Caesar

ACT I, SCENE 1

Rome, a street.

[Enter FLAVIUS, MARULLUS, and certain commoners over the stage]

FLAVIUS	Hence! home, you idle creatures, get you home!
	Is this a holiday? What, know you not,
	Being mechanical, you ought not to walk
	Upon a labouring day without the sign
	Of your profession? Speak, what trade art thou? 5
CARPENTER	Why sir, a carpenter.
MARULLUS	Where is thy leather apron and thy rule?
	What dost thou with thy best apparel on?
	You, sir, what trade are you?
COBBLER	Truly sir, in respect of a fine workman, I am but, 10
	as you would say, a cobbler.
MARULLUS	But what trade art thou? Answer me directly.
COBBLER	A trade, sir, that I hope I may use with a
	safe conscience, which is indeed, sir, a mender of 15
	bad soles.
FLAVIUS	What trade, thou knave? Thou naughty
	knave, what trade?
COBBLER	Nay, I beseech you sir, be not out with me,
	yet if thou be out, sir, I can mend you. 20
MARULLUS	What mean'st thou by that? Mend me,
	thou saucy fellow?
COBBLER	Why, sir, cobble you.
FLAVIUS	Thou art a cobbler, art thou?
COBBLER	Truly sir, all that I live by is with the awl. 25
	I meddle with no tradesman's matters nor women's
	matters, but withal—I am indeed, sir, a surgeon to
	old shoes. When they are in great danger, I recover
	them. As proper men as ever trod upon neat's leather
	have gone upon my handiwork. 30
FLAVIUS	But wherefore art not in thy shop to-day?
	Why dost thou lead these men about the streets?

ACT I, SCENE 1

Rome, a street.

[Enter FLAVIUS, MARULLUS, and certain commoners over the stage]

FLAVIUS   Go away, you lazy Romans, go home! Are you taking a holiday? Are you so ignorant that you walk the streets on a workday without your work clothes? Tell me, what is your trade?

CARPENTER   Sir, I'm a carpenter.

MARULLUS   Where is your leather apron and your tape measure? Why are you wearing your best clothes? You, what is your trade?

COBBLER   Indeed, sir, I am a cobbler.

MARULLUS   But what is your trade? Answer in simple terms.

COBBLER   A trade that suits a clear conscience—I mend wornout soles.

FLAVIUS   What is your trade, you rascal? You smirking rogue, what is your trade?

COBBLER   Please sir, don't scold me. But if you are "out" at the toes, I can repair you.

MARULLUS   What do you mean by that? How can you repair me, you impertinent fool?

COBBLER   Why, sir, I can fix you.

FLAVIUS   So you're a shoe repairman, are you?

COBBLER   Indeed sir, I earn my living by working with a sharp-pointed awl. I meddle in no business issues nor women's concerns, but with all. I am, in other words, a shoe sur-geon. When shoes are in danger, I re-sole them. The finest oxhide worn by aristocrats has required my work.

FLAVIUS   Why aren't you working today? Why are you leading workers along the streets?

COBBLER	Truly sir, to wear out their shoes, to get
	myself into more work. But indeed sir, we make
	holiday to see Caesar and to rejoice in his triumph. 35

MARULLUS	Wherefore rejoice? What conquest brings he home?
	What tributaries follow him to Rome,
	To grace in captive bonds his chariot wheels?
	You blocks, you stones, you worse than senseless things!
	O you hard hearts, you cruel men of Rome! 40
	Knew you not Pompey? Many a time and oft
	Have you climbed up to walls and battlements,
	To towers and windows, yea, to chimney tops,
	Your infants in your arms, and there have sat
	The livelong day, with patient expectation, 45
	To see great Pompey pass the streets of Rome.
	And when you saw his chariot but appear,
	Have you not made an universal shout,
	That Tiber trembled underneath her banks
	To hear the replication of your sounds 50
	Made in her concave shores?
	And do you now put-on your best attire?
	And do you now cull out a holiday?
	And do you now strew flowers in his way
	That comes in triumph over Pompey's blood? 55
	Be gone!
	Run to your houses, fall upon your knees,
	Pray to the gods to intermit the plague
	That needs must light on this ingratitude.

FLAVIUS	Go, go, good countrymen, and for this fault 60
	Assemble all the poor men of your sort;
	Draw them to Tiber banks, and weep your tears
	Into the channel, till the lowest stream
	Do kiss the most exalted shores of all.
	[Exeunt the commoners]
	See, whe'r their basest mettle be not moved. 65
	They vanish tongue-tied in their guiltiness.
	Go you down that way towards the Capitol;
	This way will I. Disrobe the images
	If you do find them decked with ceremonies.

COBBLER	If they walk on the streets and wear out their shoes, I make more jobs for myself. We are taking a holiday to see Julius Caesar and to rejoice in his triumphal parade.
MARULLUS	Why are you celebrating? What territory has he conquered for Rome? What conquered people follow him to the city? What prisoners of war are tied to his chariot wheels? You blockheads, you lumps, you ignoramuses! You insensitive clods, you cruel Romans! Don't you remember Pompey? Many times, you have climbed to the top of walls and fortresses, towers and windows, even to chimney tops, carrying your babies, and have sat a whole day waiting to see Pompey pass through Roman streets. When you glimpsed his chariot, did you not raise a shout along the way that jolted the Tiber River? Why do you dress up today? Why are you making this a holiday? Are you spreading flowers over the path of Pompey's conqueror? Scram! Run home, kneel, and pray that the gods will ward off the disease that strikes ungrateful people.
FLAVIUS	Go, good citizens, and for your sin, convene a gathering of other tradesmen. Invite them to the banks of the Tiber River to weep until the water rises to its highest mark. *[The common workers go out]* Look, they don't seem to care. They creep away tongued-tied and guilty. You go that direction towards the Capitol building. I will go this way. If you find the statues decorated, pull down the wreaths and garlands.

TRANSLATION

MARULLUS	May we do so?	70
	You know it is the feast of Lupercal.	
FLAVIUS	It is no matter. Let no images	
	Be hung with Caesar's trophies. I'll about	
	And drive away the vulgar from the streets.	
	So do you too, where you perceive them thick.	75
	These growing feathers, plucked from Caesar's wing	
	Will make him fly an ordinary pitch,	
	Who else would soar above the view of men	
	And keep us all in servile fearfulness.	
	[Exeunt]	

MARULLUS   Is that safe? You know today is the feast of Lupercal, a day to honor Rome's legendary founding.

FLAVIUS   It doesn't matter. Remove all celebrations of Caesar's triumphs from the statues. I'll force the common people from the streets. You do the same where you find them congregating. These growing fans, when removed from Caesar's procession, will bring him down to ordinary status. He wants to soar above the citizens and terrify us into groveling servants. *[They go out]*

ACT I, SCENE 2

Rome, a public place.

[Flourish. Enter CAESAR, ANTONY (for the course), CALPURNIA, PORTIA, DECIUS, CICERO, BRUTUS, CASSIUS, CASCA, a great crowd following, among them a Soothsayer; after them, MARULLUS and FLAVIUS]

CAESAR	Calpurnia.
CASCA	Peace, ho! Caesar speaks.
CAESAR	Calpurnia.
CALPURNIA	Here, my lord.
CAESAR	Stand you directly in Antonius' way When he doth run his course. Antonius.
ANTONY	Caesar, my lord?
CAESAR	Forget not in your speed, Antonius, To touch Calpurnia; for our elders say The barren, touched in this holy chase, Shake off their sterile curse.
ANTONY	I shall remember When Caesar says 'Do this,' it is performed.
CAESAR	Set on, and leave no ceremony out. *[Flourish]*
SOOTHSAYER	Caesar!
CAESAR	Ha! Who calls?
CASCA	Bid every noise be still. Peace yet again!
CAESAR	Who is it in the press that calls on me? I hear a tongue shriller than all the music Cry 'Caesar!' Speak. Caesar is turn'd to hear.
SOOTHSAYER	Beware the ides of March.
CAESAR	What man is that?
BRUTUS	A soothsayer bids you beware the ides of March.
CAESAR	Set him before me; let me see his face.
CASSIUS	Fellow, come from the throng; look upon Caesar.

Line numbers: 5, 10, 15, 20

ORIGINAL

ACT I, SCENE 2

Rome, a public place.

[A trumpet fanfare. Entering are CAESAR, ANTONY (dressed to run the race) CALPURNIA, PORTIA, DECIUS, CICERO, BRUTUS, CASSIUS, CASCA. Following are throngs of people, including a fortune teller. Behind the procession are MARULLUS and FLAVIUS]

CAESAR	Come here, Calpurnia.
CASCA	Silence. Caesar is speaking.
CAESAR	Come here, Calpurnia.
CALPURNIA	Here I am, my lord.
CAESAR	Stand in the path of Antony when he runs the race. Antony.
ANTONY	Did you call, Caesar?
CAESAR	Antony, during the race, don't forget to tap Calpurnia. Wise men say that touching women who have no children helps them to conceive.
ANTONY	I will remember. When Caesar gives an order, it is obeyed.
CAESAR	Continue and don't omit any part of the ritual. *[A trumpet fanfare]*
SOOTHSAYER	Caesar!
CAESAR	Halt. Who is calling me?
CASCA	Everybody be quiet. Hush!
CAESAR	Who is that voice in the mob that is calling me? I hear a shrill voice above the music calling "Caesar!" I am looking for the person who calls.
SOOTHSAYER	March 15 is an unlucky day.
CAESAR	Identify that man!
BRUTUS	A fortune teller says that March 15 is unlucky.
CAESAR	Bring him here. I want to look at him.
CASSIUS	You, fortune teller, step out in front of Caesar.

CAESAR	What say'st thou to me now? Speak once again.
SOOTHSAYER	Beware the ides of March.
CAESAR	He is a dreamer. Let us leave him. Pass.
	[Sennet. Exeunt all except BRUTUS and CASSIUS]
CASSIUS	Will you go see the order of the course? 25
BRUTUS	Not I.
CASSIUS	I pray you do.
BRUTUS	I am not gamesome. I do lack some part
	Of that quick spirit that is in Antony.
	Let me not hinder, Cassius, your desires. 30
	I'll leave you.
CASSIUS	Brutus, I do observe you now of late;
	I have not from your eyes that gentleness
	And show of love as I was wont to have.
	You bear too stubborn and too strange a hand 35
	Over your friend that loves you.
BRUTUS	Cassius,
	Be not deceived. If I have veiled my look,
	I turn the trouble of my countenance
	Merely upon myself. Vexed I am
	Of late with passions of some difference, 40
	Conceptions only proper to myself,
	Which give some soil, perhaps, to my behaviors;
	But let not therefore my good friends be grieved
	(Among which number, Cassius, be you one)
	Nor construe any further my neglect 45
	Than that poor Brutus, with himself at war,
	Forgets the shows of love to other men.
CASSIUS	Then, Brutus, I have much mistook your passion;
	By means whereof this breast of mine hath buried
	Thoughts of great value, worthy cogitations. 50
	Tell me, good Brutus, can you see your face?
BRUTUS	No, Cassius; for the eye sees not itself
	But by reflection, by some other things.

CAESAR	What did you predict? Tell me again.
SOOTHSAYER	March 15 is an unlucky day.
CAESAR	He is a dreamer. Let us leave him. Pass. He lives in a fantasy world. Ignore him. Pass on. *[A trumpet call. All go out except BRUTUS and CASSIUS]*
CASSIUS	Are you attending the race?
BRUTUS	No.
CASSIUS	Please do.
BRUTUS	I don't care for sports. I am not like Antony, who enjoys competition. Don't let me keep you, Cassius. Go on to the race.
CASSIUS	Brutus, I have been watching you lately. Your eyes are not so friendly and serene as they used to be. You seem obstinate and hard-handed to a man who was once your friend.
BRUTUS	Cassius, don't misinterpret my expressions. If I seem preoccupied, Cassius, it comes from being concerned with personal matters. I am disturbed lately by conflicting emotions concerning myself. These thoughts make me seem out of sorts. I don't want my friends to feel slighted. (You are among them, Cassius.) Don't misunderstand my moping. Brutus is merely battling with himself.
CASSIUS	Brutus, I have mistaken your depression. Because of your dark mood, I have not disclosed important thoughts and ideas. Brutus, can you look at your own face?
BRUTUS	No, Cassius. The only way to look at my own face is with a mirror.

CASSIUS   'Tis just.
               And it is very much lamented, Brutus,   55
               That you have no such mirrors as will turn
               Your hidden worthiness into your eye,
               That you might see your shadow. I have heard
               Where many of the best respect in Rome,
               (Except immortal Caesar), speaking of Brutus,   60
               And groaning underneath this age's yoke,
               Have wished that noble Brutus had his eyes.

BRUTUS   Into what dangers would you lead me, Cassius,
               That you would have me seek into myself
               For that which is not in me?   65

CASSIUS   Therefore, good Brutus, be prepared to hear;
               And since you know you cannot see yourself
               So well as by reflection, I, your glass,
               Will modestly discover to yourself
               That of yourself which you yet know not of.   70
               And be not jealous on me, gentle Brutus.
               Were I a common laughter, or did use
               To stale with ordinary oaths my love
               To every new protester; if you know
               That I do fawn on men and hug them hard,   75
               And after scandal them; or if you know
               That I profess myself in banqueting
               To all the rout, then hold me dangerous.
               [Flourish and shout]

BRUTUS   What means this shouting? I do fear the people
               Choose Caesar for their king.

CASSIUS   Ay, do you fear it?   80
               Then must I think you would not have it so.

BRUTUS   I would not Cassius; yet I love him well.
               But wherefore do you hold me here so long?
               What is it that you would impart to me?
               If it be aught toward the general good,   85
               Set honour in one eye and death i' th' other,
               And I will look on both indifferently;
               For let the gods so speed me as I love
               The name of honour more than I fear death.

CASSIUS	Exactly. I regret, Brutus, that there are no mirrors that will show you your good qualities. I have heard many respectable Romans (except Caesar) admiring you, Brutus. These Romans suffer from the miseries of the day. They wish that you would notice their pain.
BRUTUS	Toward what dangers are you directing me, Cassius. Why do you want me to find in my character something that doesn't exist?
CASSIUS	Let me tell you, Brutus. I will be your mirror and, without exaggerating, show you qualities that you are not aware of. Don't be suspicious of my motive, Brutus. I'm not the usual flatterer who wearies every new acquaintance with shallow claims of friendship. Don't think that I make friends, then spread rumors about them. If you think that I am too jovial at banquets with all guests, then consider me unreliable. *[A trumpet fanfare and shout]*
BRUTUS	Why is the crowd shouting? I am afraid the citizens want Caesar to be king.
CASSIUS	Are you afraid? Then I suppose that you would not want a king for Rome.
BRUTUS	I don't want a king, Cassius, but I am fond of Caesar. Why are you keeping me here in conversation? What do you want to tell me? If he has any intention other than bene-fit to Rome, I would be impartial. Let the gods know that I love honor as much as I fear death.

CASSIUS   I know that virtue to be in you, Brutus,   90
As well as I do know your outward favour.
Well, honour is the subject of my story.
I cannot tell what you and other men
Think of this life; but for my single self,
I had as lief not be as live to be   95
In awe of such a thing as I myself.
I was borne free as Caesar; so were you.
We both have fed as well, and we can both
Endure the winter's cold as well as he.
For once, upon a raw and gusty day,   100
The troubled Tiber chafing with her shores,
Caesar said to me, 'Dar'st thou, Cassius, now
Leap in with me into this angry flood
And swim to yonder point?' Upon the word,
Accoutred as I was, I plunged in   105
And bade him follow. So indeed he did.
The torrent roared, and we did buffet it
With lusty sinews, throwing it aside
And stemming it with hearts of controversy.
But ere we could arrive the point proposed,   110
Caesar cried, 'Help me Cassius, or I sink!'
I, as Aeneas, our great ancestor,
Did from the flames of Troy upon his shoulder
The old Anchises bear, so from the waves of Tiber
Did I the tired Caesar. And this man   115
Is now become a god, and Cassius is
A wretched creature and must bend his body
If Caesar carelessly but nod on him.
He had a fever when he was in Spain,
And when the fit was on him, I did mark   120
How he did shake. 'Tis true, this god did shake.
His coward lips did from their colour fly,
And that same eye whose bend doth awe the world
Did lose his lustre. I did hear him groan.
Ay, and that tongue of his that bade the Romans   125
Mark him and write his speeches in their books,
'Alas,' it cried, 'give me some drink, Titinius,'
As a sick girl! Ye gods, it doth amaze me
A man of such a feeble temper should
So get the start of the majestic world   130
And bear the palm alone.
[Shout. Flourish]

CASSIUS   I know you are a respectable man, Brutus, as well as I know your good looks. I came to talk to you about honor. I don't know what others think about life in Rome. I would rather die than stand in awe of any man. I was born free like Caesar; so were you. We have had the same upbringing and we are equally sturdy. One windy, cold day when the Tiber River was pounding the shore, Caesar said to me, "Would you join me in swimming to that distant point?" I took the dare and, fully clothed, I jumped in and called to him to follow me. He also jumped into the strong current. We swam with all our strength in the spirit of competition. Before we reached the goal, Caesar called, "Help, Cassius. I'm drowning!" Just like Aeneas, the legendary founder of Rome, bore his father Anchises on his shoulder from the burning walls of Troy, I pulled an exhausted Caesar from the Tiber. Is he worthy to be called a god? And Cassius is so unimportant that he must bow to Caesar if Caesar only nods at him. Caesar caught a fever in Spain. When spasms overtook him, I saw him trembling. It's true. This so-called god shook. His lips turned pale and the gleam disappeared from his eye, the same eye that the world honors. He groaned and—with the same tongue that commands the Romans to listen to him and make copies of his speeches—he whined, "Please, Titinius, give me a drink of water," like a sick girl! Dear God, it astonishes me that a man capable of such frailty could stand at the head of the world and rule over it. *[A shout. A trumpet fanfare]*

BRUTUS	Another general shout?
	I do believe that these applauses are
	For some new honours that are heaped on Caesar.
CASSIUS	Why, man, he doth bestride the narrow world 135
	Like a Colossus, and we petty men
	Walk under his huge legs and peep about
	To find ourselves dishonourable graves.
	Men at some time are masters of their fates.
	The fault, dear Brutus, is not in our stars, 140
	But in ourselves, that we are underlings.
	'Brutus,' and 'Caesar.' What should be in that 'Caesar'?
	Why should that name be sounded more than yours?
	Write them together: yours is as fair a name.
	Sound them: it doth become the mouth as well. 145
	Weigh them: It is as heavy. Conjure with 'em:
	'Brutus' will start a spirit as soon as 'Caesar.'
	Now in the names of all the gods at once,
	Upon what meat doth this our Caesar feed
	That he is grown so great? Age thou art shamed. 150
	Rome, thou hast lost the breed of noble bloods.
	When went there by an age since the great Flood
	But it was famed with more than with one man?
	When could they say (till now) that talked of Rome
	That her wide walks encompassed but one man? 155
	Now is it Rome indeed, and room enough,
	When there is in it but one only man.
	O, you and I have heard our fathers say
	There was a Brutus once that would have brooked
	Th' eternal devil to keep his state in Rome 160
	As easily as a king.
BRUTUS	That you do love me I am nothing jealous.
	What you would work me to, I have some aim.
	How I have thought of this, and of these times,
	I shall recount hereafter. For this present, 165
	I would not so (with love I might entreat you)
	Be any further moved. What you have said
	I will consider; what you have to say
	I will with patience hear, and find a time
	Both meet to hear and answer such high things. 170
	Till then, my noble friend, chew upon this:
	Brutus had rather be a villager
	Than to repute himself a son of Rome
	Under these hard conditions as this time
	Is like to lay upon us.

BRUTUS   What was that shout? I think the onlookers are conferring new honors on Caesar.

CASSIUS   Why, he strides across the world like the Colossus, a statue of Apollo at Rhodes. We ordinary people creep about at his feet and go to our graves without honor. At some point, all people have control of their destiny. Our fault, Brutus, is not our fate but in our unwillingness to choose our own path. The names "Brutus" and "Caesar" are not so different from each other. Why do people call out "Caesar" rather than "Brutus"? Write them out. Yours is as good a name. Pronounce them. They sound like equals. Weigh them. They weigh the same. "Brutus" is as noteworthy as "Caesar." What has Caesar done to deserve such greatness? This era is shameful. Rome, you have stopped producing great nobles. When has there ever been an age that was dominated by a single man? At what time (before now) have Romans had only one hero? Rome currently has room for only one leader. You and I have heard from our ancestors that there was once a hero named Lucius Junius Brutus who would have challenged the devil to keep out a king.

BRUTUS   I don't doubt that you admire me. What you are hinting at, I am already considering. Later, I will tell you how I have pondered Caesar's rise to greatness and the glory he bears in Rome. At the moment, I beg you, I don't want to express my emotions. I will think over what you have said. I will listen to your opinion later. I will choose a time when we can discuss such explosive ideas. Until then, my friend, think about this: Brutus would rather be a commoner than to think of himself as a noble citizen living under tyranny.

CASSIUS	I am glad 175 That my weak words have struck but thus much show Of fire from Brutus. *[Enter CAESAR and his train]*
BRUTUS	The games are done, and Caesar is returning.
CASSIUS	As they pass by, pluck Casca by the sleeve, And he will (after his sour fashion) tell you 180 What hath proceeded worthy note to-day.
BRUTUS	I will do so. But look you, Cassius, The angry spot doth glow on Caesar's brow, And all the rest look like a chidden train. Calpurnia's cheek is pale, and Cicero 185 Looks with such ferret and such fiery eyes As we have seen him in the Capitol, Being crossed in conference by some senators.
CASSIUS	Casca will tell us what the matter is.
CAESAR	Antonius. 190
ANTONY	Caesar?
CAESAR	Let me have men about me that are fat, Sleek-headed men, and such as sleep a-nights. Yond Cassius has a lean and hungry look. He thinks too much. Such men are dangerous. 195
ANTONY	Fear him not Caesar; he's not dangerous. He is a noble Roman, and well given.

CASSIUS   I am glad that my words moved you to speak so earnestly. *[Enter CAESAR and his followers]*

BRUTUS   Caesar is returning from the races.

CASSIUS   As his followers pass by, pull Casca's sleeve. He will inform you (in his cynical fashion) what happened at the assembly.

BRUTUS   I will ask him. Look, Cassius, at the angry red spot on Caesar's forehead. His followers look like they have been scolded. Calpurnia is pale and Cicero has the same angry, beady eyes that he has when senators argue with him at the Capitol.

CASSIUS   Casca will tell us what happened.

CAESAR   Antony.

ANTONY   Sir?

CAESAR   Let me have contented men about me. Cassius looks sneaky. He plots too much. Such men are dangerous.

ANTONY   Don't worry about him, Caesar. He's not dangerous. He is a good and courteous patriot.

CAESAR	Would he were fatter! But I fear him not.
	Yet if my name were liable to fear,
	I do not know the man I should avoid 200
	So soon as that spare Cassius. He reads much,
	He is a great observer, and he looks
	Quite through the deeds of men. He loves no plays
	As thou dost, Antony; he hears no music.
	Seldom he smiles, and smiles in such a sort 205
	As if he mocked himself and scorned his spirit
	That could be moved to smile at anything.
	Such men as he be never at heart's ease
	Whiles they behold a greater than themselves,
	And therefore are they very dangerous. 210
	I rather tell thee what is to be feared
	Than what I fear; for always I am Caesar.
	Come on my right hand, for this ear is deaf,
	And tell me truly what thou think'st of him.
	[Sennet. Exeunt CAESAR and his train. CASCA remains]
CASCA	You pulled me by the cloak. Would you speak with me? 215
BRUTUS	Ay, Casca. Tell us what hath chanced to-day
	That Caesar looks so sad.
CASCA	Why, you were with him, were you not?
BRUTUS	I should not then ask Casca what had chanced.
CASCA	Why, there was a crown offered him; and 220
	being offered him, he put it by the back of his hand
	thus; and then the people fell a-shouting.
BRUTUS	What was the second noise for?
CASCA	Why, for that too.
CASSIUS	They shouted thrice. What was the last cry for? 225
CASCA	Why, for that too.
BRUTUS	Was the crown offered him thrice?
CASCA	Ay, marry was't! and he put it by thrice,
	every time gentler than other; and at every putting-
	by mine honest neighbours shouted. 230
CASSIUS	Who offered him the crown?
CASCA	Why, Antony.
BRUTUS	Tell us the manner of it, gentle Casca.

CAESAR   I wish he were more content! But I'm not afraid of him. If I were easily frightened, I don't know anyone who would scare me more than that sneaky Cassius. He reads a lot, he watches other people, and he analyzes their behavior. He doesn't like drama as you do, Antony. He doesn't care for music. He seldom smiles. When he does, he appears to ridicule himself for smiling. Such men are always disgruntled while they observe anyone more powerful. Therefore, he is dangerous. I am telling you what other people fear. As for Caesar, he has no fear. Come to my right side, for the left ear is deaf. Tell me what you really think of Cassius. *[A trumpet call. CAESAR and his followers depart. CASCA remains]*

CASCA   You pulled my coat. Did you want to talk to me?

BRUTUS   Yes, Casca. We want to know what made Caesar look sad.

CASCA   Weren't you with him?

BRUTUS   If I had been with him, I wouldn't need to ask you what happened.

CASCA   He was offered a crown and refused it with the back of his hand. The audience began shouting.

BRUTUS   What caused the second outcry?

CASCA   The same thing.

CASSIUS   What caused the third cry?

CASCA   The same thing.

BRUTUS   Did he receive three offers of a crown?

CASCA   Yes, he did. And three times he refused it, but a little less sincerely each time. At each gesture, Romans shouted.

CASSIUS   Who offered Caesar the crown?

CASCA   It was Antony.

BRUTUS   Tell us the circumstances, Casca.

CASCA	I can as well be hanged as tell the manner of it. It was mere foolery; I did not mark it. I saw 235 Mark Antony offer him a crown—yet 'twas not a crown neither, 'twas one of these coronets—and, as I told you, he put it by once; but for all that, to my thinking, he would fain have had it. Then he offered it to him again; then he put it by again; but to my 240 thinking, he was very loath to lay his fingers off it. And then he offered it the third time. He put it the third time by; and still as he refused it, the rabble- ment hooted, and clapped their chopt hands, and threw tip their sweaty nightcaps, and uttered such a 245 deal of stinking breath because Caesar refused the crown that it had almost choked Caesar; for he swounded and fell down at it. And for mine own part, I durst not laugh, for fear of opening my lips and receiving the bad air. 250
CASSIUS	But soft, I pray you. What, did Caesar swound?
CASCA	He fell down in the market place and foamed at the mouth and was speechless.
BRUTUS	'Tis very like; he hath the falling sickness.
CASSIUS	No, Caesar hath it not; but you and I, 255 And honest Casca, we have the falling sickness.
CASCA	I know not what you mean by that, but I am sure Caesar fell down. If the rag-tag people did not clap him and hiss him, according as he pleased and displeased them, as they use to do the players 260 in the theatre, I am no true man.
BRUTUS	What said he when he came unto himself?

ACT I

CASCA	I don't remember. It was nonsense. I didn't pay any attention to it. I saw Mark Antony offer him a crown—it wasn't really a crown. It was a slender coronet—and, as I said, he refused it. For all the drama, I think he would gladly have taken it. Then Antony offered it to Caesar a second time. Again, Caesar refused it. In my opinion, he didn't want to take his hands off of it. Then Antony offered it to him a third time. He rejected it the third time. Because he refused it, the commoners yelled and clapped their chapped hands and tossed their sweaty hats. They exhaled so much stinking breath at Caesar's refusals that they nearly choked him. He fainted and collapsed. I wanted to laugh, but I didn't want to breathe the foul air.
CASSIUS	Halt, please. Did Caesar faint?
CASCA	He collapsed in the market and foamed at the mouth and could say nothing.
BRUTUS	It's not unusual. He has epilepsy.
CASSIUS	No, it isn't Caesar who falls down. It's you and I, Casca, who tend to fall down.
CASCA	I don't know what you mean, but I am certain that Caesar fainted. I would be lying if I didn't say that the ragtag commoners clapped and hissed, depending on whether they agreed or not. They behaved as though they were watching a play.
BRUTUS	What did Caesar say when he revived?

CASCA	Marry, before he fell down, when lie perceived the common herd was glad he refused the crown, he plucked me ope his doublet and offered them his throat to cut. An I had been a man of any occupation, if I would not have taken him at a word, I would I might go to hell among the rogues. And so he fell. When he came to himself again, he said, if he had done or said anything amiss, he desired their worships to think it was his infirmity. Three or four wenches where I stood cried 'Alas, good soul!' and forgave him with all their hearts. But there's no heed to be taken of them. If Caesar had stabbed their mothers, they would have done no less.

265

270

275

BRUTUS   And after that, he came thus sad away?

CASCA   Ay.

CASSIUS   Did Cicero say anything?

CASCA   Ay, he spoke Greek.

CASSIUS   To what effect?   280

CASCA   Nay, an I tell you that, I'll ne'er look you i'
the face again. But those that understood him
smiled at one another and shook their heads; but
for mine own part, it was Greek to me. I could tell
you more news too. Marullus and Flavius, for   285
pulling scarfs off Caesar's images, are put to silence.
Fare you well. There was more foolery yet, if I could
remember it.

CASSIUS   Will you sup with me to-night, Casca?

CASCA   No, I am promised forth.   290

CASSIUS   Will you dine with me to-morrow?

CASCA   Ay, if I be alive, and your mind hold, and
your dinner worth eating.

CASSIUS   Good. I will expect you.

CASCA   Do so. Farewell both. *[Exit]*   295

BRUTUS   What a blunt fellow is this grown to be!
He was quick mettle when he went to school.

CASCA	Before he collapsed, when he realized that the commoners were glad that he didn't want to be king, he asked me to open his vest and he offered them his throat to cut. If I had been a common laborer, I would have been convinced by Caesar's words. Then he collapsed. When he revived, he said that, if he had done or said anything wrong, he wished all to assume it was the result of his epilepsy. Three or four girls standing near me said, "Alas, good soul" and sincerely forgave him. But there is no reason to believe their words. If Caesar had stabbed their mothers, they would have forgiven him.
BRUTUS	After that, did he seem sad?
CASCA	Yes.
CASSIUS	Did Cicero say anything important?
CASCA	Yes, he spoke in Greek.
CASSIUS	What was Cicero's opinion?
CASCA	I can't tell you or I would be lying. Those people who understand Greek smiled and shook their heads; but for me, it was a foreign language. I have more news. Marullus and Flavius were executed for pulling decorations off Caesar's likenesses. Goodbye. There was more nonsense, if I could recall it.
CASSIUS	Will you dine with me tonight, Casca?
CASCA	No, I have other plans.
CASSIUS	Will you come to dinner tomorrow night?
CASCA	Yes, if I live that long and you still want me to come and you serve something good.
CASSIUS	Good. I look forward to it.
CASCA	I will be there. Goodbye to you both. *[He goes out]*
BRUTUS	He has become quite blunt. He was sharp during our school days.

CASSIUS
So is he now in execution
Of any bold or noble enterprise,
However he puts on this tardy form.   300
This rudeness is a sauce to his good wit,
Which gives men stomach to digest his words
With better appetite.

BRUTUS
And so it is. For this time I will leave you.
To-morrow, if you please to speak with me,   305
I will come home to you; or if you will,
Come home to me, and I will wait for you.

CASSIUS
I will do so. Till then, think of the world.
[Exit BRUTUS]
Well, Brutus, thou art noble; yet I see
Thy honourable mettle may be wrought   310
From that it is disposed. Therefore it is meet
That noble minds keep ever with their likes;
For who so firm that cannot be seduced?
Caesar doth bear me hard; but he loves Brutus.
If I were Brutus now and he were Cassius,   315
He should not humour me. I will this night,
In several hands, in at his windows throw,
As if they came from several citizens,
Writings, all tending to the great opinion
That Rome holds of his name; wherein obscurely   320
Caesar's ambition shall be glanced at.
And after this let Caesar seat him sure,
For we will shake him, or worse days endure. *[Exit]*

CASSIUS   Even though he pretends to be lax, he is still sharp when it comes to bold plans. His rudeness suits his wit. It allows hearers to absorb his words more easily.

BRUTUS   You're right. I will leave you for now. Tomorrow, if you still want a conversation, I will come to your house or, if you prefer, come to my house. I await your choice.

CASSIUS   Agreed. Till then, think about the world's needs. *[BRUTUS goes out]* Well, Brutus, you are a respectable man. Still, I notice that your honor can be reshaped. Therefore, it is a good idea for us to meet. No one is so pure that he can't be deceived. Caesar has a bad opinion of me; but he likes Brutus. If I were Brutus, I wouldn't let Cassius toy with my thoughts. Tonight, I will toss into his window notes composed in different handwriting that will express Rome's admiration for Brutus. The notes will imply that Caesar is too ambitious. From this day on, let Caesar watch out. We will unseat him or live through worse tyranny. *[He goes out]*

ACT I, SCENE 3

Rome, a street.

[Thunder and lightning. Enter, from opposite sides, CASCA with his sword drawn, and CICERO]

CICERO
Good even, Casca. Brought you Caesar home?
Why are you breathless? and why stare you so?

CASCA
Are you not moved when all the sway of earth
Shakes like a thing infirm? O Cicero,
I have seen tempests when the scolding winds   5
Have rived the knotty oaks, and I have seen
Th' ambitious ocean swell and rage and foam
To be exalted with the threat'ning clouds;
But never till to-night, never till now,
Did I go through a tempest dropping fire.   10
Either there is a civil strife in heaven,
Or else the world, too saucy with the gods,
Incenses them to send destruction.

CICERO
Why, saw you anything more wonderful?

CASCA
A common slave (you know him well by sight)   15
Held up his left hand, which did flame and burn
Like twenty torches joined; and yet his hand,
Not sensible of fire, remained unscorched.
Besides (I ha' not since put up my sword),
Against the Capitol I met a lion,   20
Who glazed upon me, and went surly by
Without annoying me. And there were drawn
Upon a heap a hundred ghastly women,
Transformed with their fear, who swore they saw
Men, all in fire, walk up and down the streets.   25
And yesterday the bird of night did sit
Even at noonday upon the market place,
Hooting and shrieking. When these prodigies
Do so conjointly meet, let not men say
'These are their reasons—they are natural,'   30
For I believe they are portentous things
Unto the climate that they point upon.

ORIGINAL

ACT I, SCENE 3

Rome, a street.

[Thunder and lightning. Enter, from opposite sides, CASCA with his sword drawn, and CICERO]

CICERO   Good evening, Casca. Did you escort Caesar to his home? Why are you out of breath? Why are you wide-eyed?

CASCA   Aren't you afraid when a storm shakes the ground? Cicero, I have seen strong wind split oak trees, and I have seen the ocean rage and foam under threatening skies. But this is the first time I have seen a storm dropping such lightning. Either heaven is disturbed or the world, from irreverence to the gods, angers them so much that it would destroy the earth.

CICERO   Did you see anything strange?

CASCA   A slave (someone you would recognize), held up his left hand, which seemed to blaze like the fire of 20 torches. But his hand felt no pain and remained unharmed. In addition (I was still clutching my sword), near the Capitol, I saw a lion that stared at me and went snarling by without harming me. One hundred astonished women gathered in fear. They swore they saw men on fire walk the streets. Yesterday at noon, an owl perched in the market and hooted and shrieked. When such omens occur at the same time, people can't dismiss them as normal. I believe that they are signs of our troubled times.

CICERO	It is indeed a strange-disposed time But men may construe things after their fashion, Clean from the purpose of the things themselves. 35 Comes Caesar to the Capitol to-morrow?
CASCA	He doth; for he did bid Antonius Send word to you he would be there to-morrow.
CICERO	Good night then, Casca. This disturb'd sky Is not to walk in.
CASCA	Farewell, Cicero. *[Exit CICERO]* 40 *[Enter CASSIUS]*
CASSIUS	Who's there?
CASCA	A Roman
CASSIUS	Casca, by your voice.
CASCA	Your ear is good. Cassius, what night is this!
CASSIUS	A very pleasing night to honest men.
CASCA	Who ever knew the heavens menace so?
CASSIUS	Those that have known the earth so full of faults. 45 For my part, I have walked about the streets, Submitting me unto the perilous night, And, thus unbraced, Casca, as you see, Have bared my bosom to the thunder-stone; And when the cross blue lightning seemed to open 50 The breast of heaven, I did present myself Even in the aim and very flash of it.
CASCA	But wherefore did you so much tempt the heavens? It is the part of men to fear and tremble When the most mighty gods by tokens send 55 Such dreadful heralds to astonish us.

CICERO	It is a difficult time. But people often interpret unusual events to suit their own thoughts. Is Caesar coming to the Capitol tomorrow?
CASCA	Yes. He asked Antony to report to you that he would be there.
CICERO	Good night, Casca. This turbulent weather is dangerous to pedestrians.
CASCA	Goodbye, Cicero. *[CICERO goes out] [Enter CASSIUS]*
CASSIUS	Who are you?
CASCA	A citizen.
CASSIUS	Casca, I recognize your voice.
CASCA	You have good hearing. Cassius, what a night we are having!
CASSIUS	The turbulence suits men who have nothing to hide.
CASCA	When was the weather so menacing?
CASSIUS	It seems appropriate to people who disapprove of our faulty times. As for me, I have walked the streets in this storm without a coat. Casca, as you see, I have risked being stricken by lightning. When forked lightning streaked down from the sky, I stood in the flash.
CASCA	Why did you expose yourself to danger? It is normal for people to cower when the gods send messages to astonish us.

CASSIUS	You are dull, Casca, and those sparks of life
	That should be in a Roman you do want,
	Or else you use not. You look pale, and gaze,
	And put on fear, and cast yourself in wonder, 60
	To see the strange impatience of the heavens;
	But if you would consider the true cause—
	Why all these fires, why all these gliding ghosts,
	Why birds and beasts, from quality and kind;
	Why old men, fools, and children calculate; 65
	Why all these things change from their ordinance,
	Their natures, and preformed faculties.
	To monstrous quality—why you shall find
	That heaven hath infused them with these spirits
	To make them instruments of fear and warning 70
	Unto some monstrous state.
	Now could I, Casca, name to thee a man
	Most like this dreadful night
	That thunders, lightens, opens graves, and roars
	As doth the lion in the Capitol; 75
	A man no mightier than thyself or me
	In personal action, yet prodigious grown
	And fearful, as these strange eruptions are.
CASCA	'Tis Caesar that you mean. Is it not, Cassius?
CASSIUS	Let it be who it is. For Romans now 80
	Have thews and limbs like to their ancestors;
	But woe the while! our fathers' minds are dead,
	And we are governed with other mothers' spirits;
	Our yoke and sufferance show us womanish.
CASCA	Indeed, they say the senators to-morrow 85
	Mean to establish Caesar as a king,
	And he shall wear his crown by sea and land
	In every place save here in Italy.

ACT I

CASSIUS   You are dull-witted, Casca. Either you lack true Roman courage or you conceal yours. You look pale and stare and quake and marvel at the storm. But if you analyze the cause—why these flames, ghosts, birds, and beasts act out of character, why old men, fools, and children prophesy, why all these things seem out of the ordinary— you should conclude that nature has produced monstrosities as warnings of a grotesque state of affairs. Casca, I could name a man that is as unnatural as this storm— he thunders, flashes, dishonors graves, and roars like a lion in the Capitol. This man is no stronger than you or me, but he has grown into a fierce threat, just like these strange omens.

CASCA   Are you talking about Caesar?

CASSIUS   It is who it is. Romans are no weaker than their ancestors. But, unfortunately for Rome, we have lost our masculine urges and turned into women. The fact that we allow ourselves to be bullied is womanish.

CASCA   There is a rumor that the senators will elevate Caesar to king tomorrow and that he will rule in every conquered land except Italy.

CASSIUS	I know where I will wear this dagger then;
	Cassius from bondage will deliver Cassius. 90
	Therein, ye gods, you make the weak most strong;
	Therein, ye gods, you tyrants do defeat.
	Nor stony tower, nor walls of beaten brass,
	Nor airless dungeon, nor strong links of iron,
	Can be retentive to the strength of spirit; 95
	But life, being weary of these worldly bars,
	Never lacks power to dismiss itself.
	If I know this, know all the world besides,
	That part of tyranny that I do bear
	I can shake off at pleasure. *[Thunder still]*
CASCA	So can I. 100
	So every bondman in his own hand bears
	The power to cancel his captivity.
CASSIUS	And why should Caesar be a tyrant then?
	Poor man! I know he would not be a wolf
	But that he sees the Romans are but sheep; 105
	He were no lion, were not Romans hinds.
	Those that with haste will make a mighty fire
	Behind it with weak straws. What trash is Rome,
	What rubbish and what offal, when it serves
	For the base matter to illuminate 110
	So vile a thing as Caesar! But, O grief,
	Where hast thou led me? I, perhaps, speak this
	Before a willing bondman. Then I know
	My answer must be made. But I am armed,
	And dangers are to me indifferent. 115
CASCA	You speak to Casca, and to such a man
	That is no fleering telltale. Hold, my hand.
	Be factious for redress of all these griefs,
	And I will set this foot of mine as far
	As who goes farthest. *[They shake hands]*

CASSIUS	I know where I will put my dagger. Cassius will end Cassius' life under a tyrant. You gods, through suicide, you strengthen the weak and bring down tyrants. No stone tower, no brass walls, no deep dungeon, no iron chains can confine a strong spirit. But life, which tires of tyrants, always has the power to end itself. If I accept this alternative, I can rid myself of this tyrant whenever I want. *[More thunder sounds]*
CASCA	I can do the same. Every victim has the power to escape from his captor.
CASSIUS	Then why does Caesar still rule like a tyrant? He would not act like a wolf if Romans didn't behave like sheep. He couldn't be a lion if Romans were not deer. Those in a hurry will fuel a fire with thin straws. How can Rome be such garbage by boosting Caesar to such stardom. Where has my depression led me? I hope I am addressing a fellow victim. I know I must defend my opinions. But I am ready. I don't fear danger.
CASCA	You are talking to Casca, who is not an informer. Take my hand. Join activists who want to change things. I will venture as far as they. *[They shake hands]*

CASSIUS	There's a bargain made. 120
	Now know you, Casca, I have moved already
	Some certain of the noblest-minded Romans
	To undergo with me an enterprise
	Of honourable dangerous consequence;
	And I do know, by this, they stay for me 125
	In Pompey's Porch; for now, this fearful night,
	There is no stir or walking in the streets,
	And the complexion of the element
	Is fev'rous, like the work we have in hand,
	Most bloody, fiery, and most terrible. 130
	[Enter CINNA]
CASCA	Stand close awhile, for here comes one in haste.
CASSIUS	'Tis Cinna. I do know him by his gait.
	He is a friend. Cinna, where haste you so?
CINNA	To find out you. Who's that? Metellus Cimber?
CASSIUS	No, it is Casca, one incorporate 135
	To our attempts. Am I not stayed for, Cinna?
CINNA	I am glad on't. What a fearful night is this!
	There's two or three of us have seen strange sights.
CASSIUS	Am I not stayed for? Tell me.
CINNA	Yes, you are.
	O Cassius, if you could 140
	But win the noble Brutus to our party—
CASSIUS	Be you content. Good Cinna, take this paper
	And look you lay it in the praetor's chair,
	Where Brutus may but find it. And throw this
	In at his window. Set this up with wax 145
	Upon old Brutus' statue. All this done,
	Repair to Pompey's Porch, where you shall find us.
	Is Decius Brutus and Trebonius there?
CINNA	All but Metellus Cimber, and he's gone
	To seek you at your house. Well, I will hie 150
	And so bestow the papers as you bade me.
CASSIUS	That done, repair to Pompey's Theatre.
	[Exit CINNA]
	Come, Casca, you and I will yet ere day
	See Brutus at his house. Three parts of him
	Is ours already, and the man entire 155
	Upon the next encounter yields him ours.

CASSIUS	We have struck a bargain. Casca, I have mentioned my opinion to such noble Romans who might abet me in some dangerous plot. They are waiting for me under the colonnade of Pompey's theater. This stormy night is no more dreadful than the work we plot, which is bloody and horrifying. *[Enter CINNA]*
CASCA	Stand back. Here comes someone hurrying.
CASSIUS	It's Cinna. I recognize his walk. He is trustworthy. Cinna, where are you hurrying to?
CINNA	To locate you. Is that Metellus Cimber?
CASSIUS	No, it is Casca, who is one of us. Are they waiting for me, Cinna?
CINNA	I am glad Cassius has joined us. This is a wretched night! Two or three of our group have seen peculiar omens.
CASSIUS	Are they waiting for me?
CINNA	Yes. Oh Cassius, I hope you lure Brutus into our group.
CASSIUS	Be patient. Cinna, take this note and place it in Judge Brutus' chair where he will find it. Toss this one into his window. Stick this one with wax to Lucius Junius Brutus' statue. When you finish your errands, join us at Pompey's colonnade. Are Decius Brutus and Trebonius there already?
CINNA	Everyone is waiting except Metellus Cimber, who is looking for you at your house. I will hurry and leave the notes where you wanted them.
CASSIUS	When you finish, return to Pompey's Theatre. *[CINNA goes out]* Come with me, Casca. We will visit Brutus at his house later today. I have convinced three-fourths of him. We will win him over completely at our next meeting.

TRANSLATION

CASCA

O, he sits high in all the people's hearts;
And that which would appear offence in us,
His countenance, like richest alchemy,
Will change to virtue and to worthiness.   160

CASSIUS

Him and his worth and our great need of him
You have right well conceited. Let us go,
For it is after midnight; and ere day
We will awake him and be sure of him. *[Exeunt]*

CASCA   The people admire him. His good reputation will alter the crime of our plot into a worthy deed.

CASSIUS   You have cunningly sized up his value to us. Let's go. It is after midnight. Before daylight, we will awaken him and win him over to our plot. *[They go out]*

ACT II, SCENE 1

Brutus' orchard.

[Enter BRUTUS]

BRUTUS   What, Lucius, ho!
I cannot by the progress of the stars
Give guess how near to day. Lucius I say!
I would it were my fault to sleep so soundly.
When, Lucius, when? Awake, I say! What, Lucius!   5
[Enter LUCIUS]

LUCIUS   Called you, my lord?

BRUTUS   Get me a taper in my study, Lucius.
When it is lighted, come and call me here.

LUCIUS   I will, my lord. *[Exit]*

BRUTUS   It must be by his death; and for my part,   10
I know no personal cause to spurn at him,
But for the general. He would be crowned.
How that might change his nature, there the question.
It is the bright day that brings forth the adder,
And that craves wary walking. Crown him that   15
And then I grant we put a sting in him
That at his will he may do danger with.
Th' abuse of greatness is, when it disjoins
Remorse from power. And to speak truth of Caesar
I have not known when his affections swayed   20
More than his reason. But 'tis common proof
That lowliness is young ambition's ladder,
Whereto the climber upward turns his face;
But when lie once attains the upmost round,
He then unto the ladder turns his back,   25
Looks in the clouds, scorning the base degrees
By which he did ascend. So Caesar may.
Then lest he may, prevent. And since the quarrel
Will bear no colour for the thing he is,
Fashion it thus: that what he is, augmented,   30
Would run to these and these extremities;
And therefore think him as a serpent's egg,
Which, hatched, would as his kind grow mischievous
And kill him in the shell.
[Enter LUCIUS]

ACT II, SCENE 1

Brutus' orchard.

[Enter BRUTUS]

BRUTUS   Lucius, I need you. I cannot guess by the stars what time it is. Lucius, I'm calling you. I wish I slept as soundly as he. Where are you, Lucius? Get up! Lucius! *[Enter LUCIUS]*

LUCIUS   Did you call me, my lord?

BRUTUS   Set a candle in my study, Lucius. After you light it, call me.

LUCIUS   I will, my lord. *[He goes out]*

BRUTUS   Caesar has to die. For personal reasons, I have no cause to denounce him. It must be done for the people of Rome. He wants to be king of Rome. No one knows how a crown would change him. A bright day draws out the snake and forces us to walk carefully. A crown might give him the opportunity to strike at will. Abuse of power occurs when rulers no longer regret their faults. Truly, I have never known him to let willfulness overrule reason. But it is widely known that ambition begins as humility and grows into tyranny. Once the ambitious person climbs to the top, he forgets to acknowledge the people who made him great. This could happen with Caesar. It is better to stop him before he becomes a problem. And since the issue is not his current faults, I must look at it this way: If his current powers grow, he might become a tyrant. I should think of him as a snake's egg and kill him in the shell before he hatches into a menace. *[Enter LUCIUS]*

LUCIUS	The taper burneth in your closet, sir. 35
	Searching the window for a flint, I found
	This paper, thus sealed tip; and I am sure
	It did not lie there when I went to bed.
	[Gives him a letter]
BRUTUS	Get you to bed again; it is not day.
	Is not to-morrow, boy, the ides of March? 40
LUCIUS	I know not, sir.
BRUTUS	Look in the calendar and bring me word.
LUCIUS	I will, sir. *[Exit]*
BRUTUS	These exhalations, whizzing in the air,
	Gives so much light that I may read by them. 45
	[Opens the letter and reads]
	'Brutus, thou sleep'st. Awake and see thyself!
	Shall Rome, &c. Speak, strike, redress!'
	Brutus, thou sleep'st. Awake!
	Such instigations have been often dropped
	Where I have took them up. 50
	'Shall Rome, &c.' Thus must I piece it out:
	Shall Rome stand under one man's awe? What, Rome?
	My ancestors did from the streets of Rome
	The Tarquin drive when he was called a king.
	'Speak, strike, redress!' Am I entreated 55
	To speak and strike? O Rome, I make thee promise,
	If the redress will follow, thou receivest
	Thy full petition at the hand of Brutus.
	[Enter LUCIUS]
LUCIUS	Sir, March is wasted fifteen days.
	[Knock within]
BRUTUS	'Tis good. Go to the gate; somebody knocks. 60
	[Exit LUCIUS]
	Since Cassius first did whet me against Caesar,
	I have not slept.
	Between the acting of a dreadful thing
	And the first motion, all the interim is
	Like a phantasma or a hideous dream. 65
	The genius and the mortal instruments
	Are then in council, and the state of man,
	Like to a little kingdom, suffers then
	The nature of an insurrection.
	[Enter LUCIUS]

LUCIUS	I lit a candle in your study, sir. When I was looking for a flint to strike a light, I found this sealed note. I am sure it was not there when I went to bed. *[Gives him a letter]*
BRUTUS	Go back to bed. It is still night. Isn't tomorrow March 15?
LUCIUS	I don't know, sir.
BRUTUS	Look it up on the calendar and report to me.
LUCIUS	I will, sir. *[He departs]*
BRUTUS	This lightning sheds so much light that I can read by it. *[Opens the letter and reads]* "Brutus, wake up and examine your place in Rome! Shall Rome, etc. Raise your voice, strike out at Caesar, right these wrongs!" Such unsigned notes have often been left for me to find. "Shall Rome, etc." I must work out these clues. Shall Rome survive under a tyrant? Rome tolerate tyranny? My ancestor, Lucius Junius Brutus, drove King Tarquin from the city. "Raise your voice, strike out at Caesar, right these wrongs!" Do the authors want me to raise a rebellion? I promise you, my country, if correction is needed, I will do all you ask. *[Enter LUCIUS]*
LUCIUS	Sir, it is March 15. *[Knock within]*
BRUTUS	Thank you. See who is knocking at the gate. *[LUCIUS goes out]* Since Cassius first asked me my opinion of Caesar, I have not slept. Between the initial idea and the completion of a dreadful act, I live in an illusion or a nightmare. My spirit and my body debate. Like a small country, I endure a rebellion. *[Enter LUCIUS]*

ACT II

LUCIUS	Sir, 'tis your brother Cassius at the door, 70
	Who doth desire to see you.
BRUTUS	Is he alone?
LUCIUS	No, sir. There are moe with him.
BRUTUS	Do you know them?
LUCIUS	No, Sir. Their hats are plucked about their ears
	And half their faces buried in their cloaks,
	That by no means I may discover them 75
	By any mark of favour.
BRUTUS	Let 'em enter. *[Exit LUCIUS]*
	They are the faction. O conspiracy,
	Sham'st thou to show thy dangerous brow by night,
	When evils are most free? O, then by day
	Where wilt thou find a cavern dark enough 80
	To mask thy monstrous visage? Seek none, conspiracy.
	Hide it in smiles and affability:
	For if thou put thy native semblance on,
	Not Erebus itself were dim enough
	To hide thee from prevention. 85
	[Enter the conspirators, CASSIUS, CASCA, DECIUS,
	CINNA, METELLUS CIMBER, and TREBONIUS]
CASSIUS	I think we are too bold upon your rest.
	Good morrow, Brutus. Do we trouble you?
BRUTUS	I have been up this hour, awake all night.
	Know I these men that come along with you?
CASSIUS	Yes, every man of them; and no man here 90
	But honours you; and every one doth wish
	You had but that opinion of yourself
	Which every noble Roman bears of you.
	This is Trebonius.
BRUTUS	He is welcome hither.
CASSIUS	This, Decius Brutus.
BRUTUS	He is welcome too. 95
CASSIUS	This, Casca; this, Cinna; and this Metellus Cimber.
BRUTUS	They are all welcome.
	What watchful cares do interpose themselves
	Betwixt your eyes and night?

ORIGINAL

LUCIUS	Sir, your brother-in-law Cassius has arrived and wants to see you.
BRUTUS	Is he alone?
LUCIUS	No, sir. There are more with him.
BRUTUS	Do you recognize them?
LUCIUS	No, sir. They pull their hats down to their ears and bury half their faces in their coats so I can't see their features.
BRUTUS	Show them in. *[LUCIUS goes out]* These are the conspirators. Oh conspiracy, are you ashamed to be recognized at night, when most evil deeds are committed? Would you hide in a cave by day to conceal your ugly face? Seek no hiding place, conspirators. Conceal your plots with smiles and chatter. If you wear your normal faces, hell itself could not halt your plot. *[Enter the conspirators, CASSIUS, CASCA, DECIUS, CINNA, METELLUS CIMBER, and TREBONIUS]*
CASSIUS	I think we have disturbed you. Good morning, Brutus. Are we inconveniencing you?
BRUTUS	I have been up all night. Do I know your companions?
CASSIUS	Yes, you know each man. All of them respect you. Each man wishes that you valued your worth as much as Romans honor you. This is Trebonius.
BRUTUS	You are welcome here.
CASSIUS	This is Decius Brutus.
BRUTUS	You are also welcome.
CASSIUS	Here are Casca, Cinna, and Metellus Cimber.
BRUTUS	You are all welcome. What worries keep you up tonight?

ACT II

CASSIUS	Shall I entreat a word? *[They whisper]*	100
DECIUS	Here lies the east. Doth not the day break here?	
CASCA	No.	
CINNA	O, pardon sir, it doth; and yon grey lines That fret the clouds are messengers of day.	
CASCA	You shall confess that you are both deceived. Here, as I point my sword, the sun arises, Which is a great way growing on the south, Weighing the youthful season of the year. Some two months hence, up higher toward the north He first presents his fire; and the high east Stands as the Capitol, directly here.	105 110
BRUTUS	Give me your hands all over, one by one.	
CASSIUS	And let us swear our resolution.	
BRUTUS	No, not an oath. If not the face of men, The sufferance of our souls, the time's abuse— If these be motives weak, break off betimes, And every man hence to his idle bed. So let high-sighted tyranny rage on Till each man drop by lottery. But if these (As I am sure they do) bear fire enough To kindle cowards and to steel with valour The melting spirits of women, then, countrymen, What need we any spur but our own cause To prick us to redress? what other bond Than secret Romans that have spoke the word And will not palter? and what other oath Than honesty to honesty engaged That this shall be, or we will fall for it? Swear priests and cowards and men cautelous, Old feeble carrions and such suffering souls That welcome wrongs; unto bad causes swear Such creatures as men doubt; but do not stain The even virtue of our enterprise, Nor th' insuppressive mettle of our spirits, To think that or our cause or our performance Did need an oath; when every drop of blood That every Roman bears, and nobly bears, Is guilty of a several bastardy If he do break the smallest particle Of any promise that hath passed from him.	 115 120 125 130 135 140

ORIGINAL

CASSIUS	May I have a private word with you? *[Cassius and Brutus whisper]*
DECIUS	This is the east. Doesn't the sun rise here?
CASCA	No.
CINNA	I beg your pardon, sir, but it is daybreak. The gray streaks among the clouds precede sunrise.
CASCA	You are both wrong. The sun rises here where I point my sword. It tends toward the south in March. In May, sunrise will move higher toward the north. At the high point, it rises at the Capitol in this direction.

ACT II

BRUTUS	I want to shake each man's hand.
CASSIUS	And let us swear our intent.
BRUTUS	No, we don't need an oath. If the unhappiness in people's faces and the suffering in their souls do not attest to hard times—if these proofs are weak, we should quit now and return to bed. So let the ambitious tyrant survive and each citizen die in his own time. But if these proofs turn cowards and quitters into heroes (as I am sure they do), then, patriots, we need only the nation's cause as an excuse for our plot. What other allegiance than patriotism will strengthen us? And what other oath than honest intent shall make this happen or destroy us for attempting rebellion? Priests, cowards, and connivers and frail old men and such sufferers that encourage tyranny. The kinds of plotters that men doubt are the ones that swear oaths. Do not dishonor the purpose of our plot nor the strength of our spirits by demanding an oath. Every drop of Roman blood is guilty of treachery if anyone breaks his promise.

TRANSLATION

CASSIUS	But what of Cicero? Shall we sound him? I think he will stand very strong with us.
CASCA	Let us not leave him out.
CINNA	No, by no means.
METELLUS	O, let us have him! for his silver hairs Will purchase us a good opinion 145 And buy men's voices to commend our deeds. It shall be said his judgment ruled our hands. Our youths and wildness shall no whit appear, But all be buried in his gravity.
BRUTUS	O, name him not! Let us not break with him; 150 For he will never follow anything That other men begin.
CASSIUS	Then leave him out.
CASCA	Indeed he is not fit.
DECIUS	Shall no man else be touched but only Caesar?
CASSIUS	Decius, well urged. I think it is not meet 155 Mark Antony, so well beloved of Caesar, Should outlive Caesar. We shall find of him A shrewd contriver; and you know, his means, If he improve them, may well stretch so far As to annoy us all; which, to prevent, 160 Let Antony and Caesar fall together.

CASSIUS	What will we do about Cicero? Should we ask him to join our conspiracy? I think he will support us.
CASCA	Let's include him.
CINNA	No, not Cicero.
METELLUS	Let's invite him! His age will improve our showing among Romans and ensure us the people's approval. People will think his judgment directed us. No one will think us immature or wild. All will honor his gravity.
BRUTUS	Don't include him! Let's not inform him of our plot. He won't join anything that derives from other people's ideas.
CASSIUS	Then forget Cicero.
CASCA	He isn't suitable.
DECIUS	Shall we kill only Caesar?
CASSIUS	That's a good question, Decius. I think we should also kill Mark Antony, Caesar's cohort. Mark Antony is a shrewd man. If others follow him, we may suffer for it. To keep this from happening, let's kill Antony and Caesar at the same time.

ACT II

BRUTUS	Our course will seem too bloody, Caius Cassius,
	To cut the head off and then hack the limbs,
	Like wrath in death and envy afterwards;
	For Antony is but a limb of Caesar. 165
	Let's be sacrificers, but not butchers, Caius.
	We all stand up against the spirit of Caesar,
	And in the spirit of men there is no blood.
	O that we then could come by Caesar's spirit
	And not dismember Caesar! But, alas, 170
	Caesar must bleed for it! And, gentle friends,
	Let's kill him boldly, but not wrathfully;
	Let's carve him as a dish fit for the gods,
	Not hew him as a carcass fit for hounds.
	And let our hearts, as subtle masters do, 175
	Stir up their servants to an act of rage
	And after seem to chide 'em. This shall make
	Our purpose necessary, and not envious;
	Which so appearing to the common eyes,
	We shall be called purgers, not murderers. 180
	And for Mark Antony, think not of him;
	For he can do no more than Caesar's arm
	When Caesar's head is off.
CASSIUS	Yet I fear him;
	For in the ingrafted love he bears to Caesar—
BRUTUS	Alas, good Cassius, do not think of him! 185
	If he love Caesar, all that he can do
	Is to himself—take thought, and die for Caesar.
	And that were much he should; for he is given
	To sports, to wildness, and much company.
TREBONIUS	There is no fear in him. Let him not die; 190
	For he will live, and laugh at this hereafter.
	[Clock strikes]
BRUTUS	Peace! Count the clock.
CASSIUS	The clock hath stricken three.
TREBONIUS	'Tis time to part.

BRUTUS	Our plot will seem too violent, Caius Cassius, if we kill the tyrant, then murder his associates. We would seem envious of his followers. Antony is only one of Caesar's aides. Let's sacrifice Caesar, but not butcher his followers, Caius. We will defy only Caesar's ambition. If we could murder his ambition and not kill the man! But, unfortunately, Caesar must die if we want to kill his ambition. Good friends, let's do this boldly, but not in anger. Let's sacrifice him to the gods but not slaughter him for dogs to eat. And let our hearts, like experienced slavemasters, stir our hands to action, then force them back toward peace. We want people to perceive our purpose as necessary rather than malicious. To the ordinary Roman, we will be called rescuers, not killers. As for Mark Antony, don't give him a thought. He will be powerless once Caesar is dead.

ACT II

CASSIUS	I'm afraid of Antony for his friendship with Caesar—
BRUTUS	Cassius, forget Antony! If he is Caesar's friend, all he can do is kill himself—he will consider his political position and die with Caesar. Which is what Antony should do. Antony favors sports, wild behavior, and carousing.
TREBONIUS	We shouldn't fear Antony. Let him live. He will eventually laugh at Caesar's assassination. *[Clock strikes]*
BRUTUS	Hush! Count the chimes.
CASSIUS	The clock has struck 3:00 a.m.
TREBONIUS	We must separate.

TRANSLATION

CASSIUS   But it is doubtful yet
                 Whether Caesar will come forth to-day or no;
                 For he is superstitious grown of late,   195
                 Quite from the main opinion he held once
                 Of fantasy, of dreams, and ceremonies.
                 It may be these apparent prodigies,
                 The unaccustomed terror of this night,
                 And the persuasion of his augurers   200
                 May hold him from the Capitol to-day.

DECIUS   Never fear that. If he be so resolved,
                 I can o'ersway him; for he loves to hear
                 That unicorns may be betrayed with trees
                 And bears with glasses, elephants with holes,   205
                 Lions with toils, and men with flatterers;
                 But when I tell him he hates flatterers,
                 He says he does, being then most flattered.
                 Let me work;
                 For I can give his humour the true bent   210
                 And I will bring him to the Capitol.

CASSIUS   Nay, we will all of us be there to fetch him.

BRUTUS   By the eighth hour. Is that the uttermost?

CINNA   Be that the uttermost, and fail not then.

METELLUS   Caius Ligarius doth bear Caesar hard,   215
                 Who rated him for speaking well of Pompey.
                 I wonder none of you have thought of him.

BRUTUS   Now, good Metellus, go along by him.
                 He loves me well, and I have given him reasons
                 Send him but hither, and I'll fashion him.   220

CASSIUS   The morning comes upon 's. We'll leave you, Brutus.
                 And, friends, disperse yourselves; but all remember
                 What we have said and show yourselves true Romans.

CASSIUS	I doubt that Caesar will appear today. He has become quite superstitious, unlike his former opinion of imagination, dreams, and rituals. It could be that these omens and this storm tonight will cause his prophets to stop him from going to the Capitol today.
DECIUS	Don't worry. If he chooses to stay home, I can persuade him. He loves to hear how unicorns can be lured to sink their horns into trees, bears can be tricked by mirrors, lions with nets, and men with flatterers. But when I flatter him that he can't be flattered, he will fall for my trick. Let me do my work. I can sway his opinion and escort him to the Capitol.
CASSIUS	No, all of us should escort him.
BRUTUS	By 8:00 a.m. Is that the best time?
CINNA	8:00 a.m. at the latest. And don't fail to join us.
METELLUS	Caius Ligarius carries a deep grudge against Caesar for chiding him for honoring Pompey. I am surprised that no one has invited him to this group.
BRUTUS	Metellus, fetch Caius Ligarius. He likes me. I will shape his opinion after he arrives.
CASSIUS	It's getting late. Goodbye, Brutus. Friends, leave separately. Remember our conspiracy and don't fail the plot.

ACT II

TRANSLATION

BRUTUS   Good gentlemen, look fresh and merrily.
                Let not our looks put on our purposes,   225
                But bear it as our Roman actors do,
                With untired spirits and formal constancy.
                And so good morrow to you every one.
                [Exeunt all except BRUTUS]
                Boy! Lucius! Fast asleep? It is no matter.
                Enjoy the honey-heavy due of slumber.   230
                Thou has no figures nor no fantasies
                Which busy care draws in the brains of men;
                Therefore thou sleep'st so sound.
                [Enter PORTIA]

PORTIA   Brutus, my lord.

BRUTUS   Portia! What mean you? Wherefore rise you now?
                It is not for your health thus to commit   235
                Your weak condition to the raw cold morning.

PORTIA   Nor for yours neither. Y' have ungently, Brutus,
                Stole from my bed. And yesternight at supper
                You suddenly arose and walked about,
                Musing and sighing with your arms across: 240
                And when I asked you what the matter was,
                You stared upon me with ungentle looks.
                I urged you further; then you scratched your head
                And too impatiently stamped with your foot.
                Yet I insisted; yet you answered not,   245
                But with an angry wafter of your hand
                Gave sign for me to leave you. So I did,
                Fearing to strengthen that impatience
                Which seemed too much enkindled, and withal
                Hoping it was but an effect of humor,   250
                Which sometime hath his hour with every man.
                It will not let you eat nor talk nor sleep,
                And could it work so much upon your shape
                As it hath much prevailed on your condition,
                I should not know you Brutus. Dear my lord,   255
                Make me acquainted with your cause of grief.

BRUTUS   I am not well in health, and that is all.

PORTIA   Brutus is wise and, were he not in health,
                He would embrace the means to come by it.

BRUTUS   Why so I do. Good Portia, go to bed.   260

BRUTUS	Gentlemen, look rested and cheerful. Let's not show our intent in our expressions. Let's bear our parts like actors who seem rested and normal. Good day to you all. *[All depart except BRUTUS]* Boy! Lucius! Gone back to sleep? That's okay. Enjoy your rest. You have no plots or imaginings that worry adults. That's why you sleep so soundly. *[Enter PORTIA]*

PORTIA	Brutus, my lord.
BRUTUS	Portia, why are you up so early? It is not good for you to arise in the cold morning.
PORTIA	Nor is it good for you. You have abruptly arisen from my bed. Last night at supper, you got up from the table, paced, and mused and sighed with your arms folded. When I asked if you were ill, you stared roughly at me. I asked you again. You scratched your head and stamped your feet. When I insisted, you said nothing, but, with an impatient wave of your hand, you sent me away. I left you alone out of fear that I would make you angrier. I hoped that your foul mood was temporary. You are too disturbed to eat, converse, or sleep. If this trouble continues, I will not recognize you as Brutus. Please my lord, tell me your troubles.
BRUTUS	I don't feel well.
PORTIA	You are wise enough to seek treatment for sickness.
BRUTUS	I am seeking treatment. Portia, go back to bed.

PORTIA   Is Brutus sick, and is it physical
                  To walk unbraced and suck up the humours
                  Of the dank morning? What, is Brutus sick,
                  And will he steal out of his wholesome bed
                  To dare the vile contagion of the night,   265
                  And tempt the rheumy and unpurged air,
                  To add unto his sickness? No, my Brutus.
                  You have some sick offence within your mind,
                  Which by the right and virtue of my place
                  I ought to know of; and upon my knees   270
                  I charm you, by my once commended beauty,
                  By all your vows of love; and that great vow
                  Which did incorporate and make us one,
                  That you unfold to me, your self, your half,
                  Why you are heavy—and what men to-night   275
                  Have had resort to you; for here have been
                  Some six or seven, who did hide their faces
                  Even from darkness.

BRUTUS   Kneel not, gentle Portia.

PORTIA   I should not need if you were gentle Brutus.
                  Within the bond of marriage, tell me, Brutus,   280
                  It is excepted I should know no secrets
                  That appertain to you? Am I your self
                  But, as it were, in sort or limitation?
                  To keep with you at meals, comfort your bed,
                  And talk to you sometimes? Dwell I but in the suburbs 285
                  Of your good pleasure? If it be no more,
                  Portia is Brutus' harlot, not his wife.

BRUTUS   You are my true and honourable wife,
                  As dear to me as are the ruddy drops
                  That visit my sad heart.   290

PORTIA   If this were true, then should I know this secret.
                  I grant I am a woman; but withal
                  A woman that Lord Brutus took to wife.
                  I grant I am a woman; but withal
                  A woman well-reputed, Cato's daughter.   295
                  Think you I am no stronger than my sex,
                  Being so fathered and so husbanded?
                  Tell me your counsels; I will not disclose 'em.
                  I have made strong proof of my constancy,
                  Giving myself a voluntary wound   300
                  Here, in the thigh. Can I bear that with patience,
                  And not my husband's secrets?

PORTIA	Are you ill? Is it healthful to walk uncloaked in the damp morning air? If you are sick, would you leave your bed and venture out in the moist, impure night air to make yourself sicker? No, Brutus, you have some worry that, as your wife, I should know about. I kneel before you and reveal the beauty that you once vowed to love. And by our marriage vows, by which you became my husband, tell me why you are depressed. What men came here tonight? I saw six or seven who hid their faces in the dark.
BRUTUS	Get up, sweet Portia.
PORTIA	I wouldn't have to kneel if you were behaving like a husband. Are you keeping secrets from me, Brutus. Does our relationship limit me? Am I your dinner partner, bed mate, and companion only sometimes? Must I exist on the outskirts of your heart? If that is my purpose, then I am your mistress, not a wife.
BRUTUS	You are my true, worthy wife, as dear to me as is the blood in my heart.
PORTIA	If I am dear to you, I should share your secrets. I know that I am only female, but I am the woman whom Brutus chose as a wife. I know that I am only female, but I am a respectable woman, daughter of Cato, Rome's moralist. Do you think I, with so noble a father and husband, am only a weakling? Tell me your secrets; I can keep them. I have demonstrated my worthiness by stabbing myself in the thigh. Can I tolerate a wound and not keep my husband's secrets?

TRANSLATION

BRUTUS	O ye gods,
	Render me worthy of this noble wife!
	[Knocking within]
	Hark! hark! One knocks. Portia, go in awhile,
	And by and by thy bosom shall partake 305
	The secrets of my heart.
	All my engagements I will construe thee,
	And all the charactery of my sad brows.
	Leave me with haste. *[Exit PORTIA]*
	Lucius, who's that knocks?
	[Enter LUCIUS and CAIUS LIGARIUS]
LUCIUS	Here is a sick man that would speak with you. 310
BRUTUS	Caius Ligarius, that Metellus spake of.
	Boy stand aside. Caius Ligarius, how?
CAIUS	Vouchsafe good morrow from a feeble tongue.
BRUTUS	O, what a time have you chose out, brave Caius,
	To wear a kerchief! Would you were not sick! 315
CAIUS	I am not sick if Brutus have in hand
	Any exploit worthy the name of honour.
BRUTUS	Such an exploit have I in hand, Ligarius,
	Had you a healthful ear to hear of it.
CASSIUS	By all the gods that Romans bow before, 320
	I here discard my sickness. *[Throws off his kerchief]*
	Soul of Rome,
	Brave son derived from honourable loins,
	Thou like an exorcist hast conjured up
	My mortified spirit. Now bid me run,
	And I will strive with things impossible; 325
	Yea, get the better of them. What's to do?
BRUTUS	A piece of work that will make sick men whole.
CAIUS	But are not some whole that we must make sick?
BRUTUS	That must we also. What it is, my Caius,
	I shall unfold to thee as we are going, 330
	To whom it must be done.
CAIUS	Set on your foot,
	And with a heart new-fired I follow you,
	To do I know not what; but it sufficeth
	That Brutus leads me on. *[Thunder]*
BRUTUS	Follow me then. *[Exeunt]* 335

ORIGINAL

BRUTUS	Oh, you Gods, make me worthy of so valuable a wife! *[Knocking within]* Listen! Someone is knocking. Portia, go back into the house. Soon, I will tell you my heart's secrets. All my meetings I will explain to you and the reason for my wrinkled brow. Leave me quickly. *[PORTIA goes out]* Lucius, who is knocking? *[Enter LUCIUS and CAIUS LIGARIUS]*
LUCIUS	There is a sick man who wants to talk to you.
BRUTUS	Caius Ligarius, whom Metellus spoke of. Boy, wait outside. Caius Ligarius, how are you?
CAIUS	Good morning from a sick tongue.
BRUTUS	What a time you have chosen, Caius, to get sick. I wish you were well!
CAIUS	I am well enough if Brutus is to strike in the name of honor.
BRUTUS	I am planning such a strike, Ligarius, if you are well enough to listen to it.
CASSIUS	By all the gods that Romans worship, I give up my bandage. *[Throws his bandage away]* You brave Roman from honorable ancestors, you have revived my sickly spirit. Now order me to run and I will do the impossible; I would even win the race. What is your plan?
BRUTUS	A piece of work that will make sick men whole. A job that will make the sick well.
CAIUS	But aren't there some who must be killed?
BRUTUS	Yes, we must. Caius, as we walk, I will tell you who must die.
CAIUS	Let's go. I will follow you with new vigor, even if I don't know what the plan is. It is enough that Brutus invites me to help. *[Thunder]*
BRUTUS	Then follow me. *[They go out]*

ACT II

TRANSLATION

ACT II, SCENE 2

Caesar's house.

[Thunder and lightning. Enter JULIUS CAESAR, in his nightgown]

CAESAR	Nor heaven nor earth have been at peace to-night.
	Thrice hath Calpurnia in her sleep cried out
	'Help ho! They murder Caesar!' Who's within?
	[Enter a Servant]
SERVANT	My lord?
CAESAR	Go bid the priests do present sacrifice, 5
	And bring me their opinions of success.
SERVANT	I will, my lord. *[Exit]*
	[Enter CALPURNIA]
CALPURNIA	What mean you Caesar? Think you to walk forth?
	You shall not stir out of your house to-day.
CAESAR	Caesar shall forth. The things that threatened me 10
	Ne'er looked but on my back. When they shall see
	The face of Caesar, they are vanished.
CALPURNIA	Caesar, I never stood on ceremonies,
	Yet now they fright me. There is one within,
	Besides the things that we have heard and seen, 15
	Recounts most horrid sights seen by the watch.
	A lioness hath whelped in the streets,
	And graves have yawned and yielded up their dead.
	Fierce fiery warriors fought upon the clouds
	In ranks and squadrons and right form of war, 20
	Which drizzled blood upon the Capitol.
	The noise of battle hurtled in the air,
	Horses did neigh, and dying men did groan,
	And ghosts did shriek and squeal about the streets.
	O Caesar, these things are beyond all use, 25
	And I do fear them!
CAESAR	What can be avoided
	Whose end is purposed by the mighty gods?
	Yet Caesar shall go forth; for these predictions
	Are to the world in general as to Caesar.
CALPURNIA	When beggars die there are no comets seen; 30
	The heavens themselves blaze forth the death of princes.

ACT II, SCENE 2

Caesar's house.

[Thunder and lightning. JULIUS CAESAR, in his nightgown, enters]

CAESAR   Neither the sky nor earth has been quiet tonight. Three times, Calpurnia has cried out in her sleep, "Help! They are murdering Caesar!" Who is there? *[Enter a Servant]*

SERVANT   My lord?

CAESAR   Go ask the priests to perform a ritual sacrifice and bring me their interpretations.

SERVANT   I will, my lord. *[He goes out] [Enter CALPURNIA]*

CALPURNIA   What are you thinking, Caesar? Are you going out today? You should stay home.

CAESAR   Caesar will go out today. Threats are behind me, not in front. When I look them in the face, they vanish.

CALPURNIA   Caesar, I never noticed omens, but now they scare me. There is someone here who has heard terrifying sights reported by the watchman. A lion gave birth in the streets, and graves opened and tossed up their dead. Flaming warriors fought in the sky in regiments as though in a war and shed blood on the Capitol. The noise of combat echoed through the air. War horses neighed, dying men groaned, and ghosts shrieked about the streets. Oh Caesar, these omens are unnatural; I am afraid.

CAESAR   How can I avoid what the gods command? I will go out today, for these omens are for the whole world, not just for Caesar.

CALPURNIA   When beggars die, there are no comets to announce their deaths. When princes die, the skies blaze.

ACT II

TRANSLATION

CAESAR	Cowards die many times before their deaths;
	The valiant never taste of death but once.
	Of all the wonders that I yet have heard,
	It seems to me most strange that men should fear, 35
	Seeing that death, a necessary end,
	Will come when it will come.
	[Enter a Servant]
	What say the augurers?
SERVANT	They would not have you to stir forth to-day.
	Plucking the entrails of an offering forth,
	They could not find a heart within the beast. 40
CAESAR	The gods do this in shame of cowardice.
	Caesar should be a beast without a heart
	If he should stay at home to-day for fear.
	No, Caesar shall not. Danger knows full well
	That Caesar is more dangerous than he. 45
	We are two lions littered in one day,
	And I the elder and more terrible,
	And Caesar shall go forth.
CALPURNIA	Alas, my lord,
	Your wisdom is consumed in confidence.
	Do not go forth to-day. Call it my fear 50
	That keeps you in the house and not your own.
	We'll send Mark Antony to the Senate House,
	And he shall say you are not well to-day.
	Let me upon my knee prevail in this.
CAESAR	Mark Antony shall say I am not well, 55
	And for thy humour I will stay at home.
	[Enter DECIUS]
	Here's Decius Brutus; he shall tell them so.
DECIUS	Caesar, all hail! Good morrow, worthy Caesar;
	I come to fetch you to the Senate House.
CAESAR	And you are come in very happy time 60
	To bear my greetings to the senators
	And tell them that I will not come to-day.
	Cannot, is false; and that I dare not, falser:
	I will not come to-day. Tell them so, Decius.
CALPURNIA	Say he is sick.

CAESAR	Cowards are constantly in fear of death. Brave people never face death until it comes. Of all the strange human quirks, I am amazed that people fear death, which is a natural and unpredictable part of life. *[Enter a Servant]* What do the prophets say?
SERVANT	They say that you should stay home today. When they disemboweled the sacrificial beast, they found no heart.
CAESAR	The gods provided this heartless sacrifice to shame cowards. I would be a heartless beast if I stayed home today. I shall not stay home. I am more dangerous than any threat. Danger and I were born on the same day. I am older and more fearful. I will go out today.
CALPURNIA	You are more confident than is wise. Please stay home. Do it because of my fear rather than for yours. Send Mark Antony to the Senate Chamber to report that you are sick. I beg you on my knees.
CAESAR	Mark Antony will take the message that I am sick. To please you, I will stay home. *[Enter DECIUS]* Here comes Decius Brutus. He will take my message.
DECIUS	Greetings, Caesar. I came to escort you to the Senate House.
CAESAR	You are just in time to tell the senators that I am staying home today. It's a lie to say I can't come. It's more false to say I dare not come. I will not come today. Give them my message, Decius.
CALPURNIA	Report that Caesar is sick.

ACT II

TRANSLATION

CAESAR	Shall Caesar send a lie?	65
	Have I in conquest stretched mine arm so far	
	To be afeard to tell greybeards the truth?	
	Decius, go tell them Caesar will not come.	

CAESAR   Shall Caesar send a lie?   65
Have I in conquest stretched mine arm so far
To be afeard to tell greybeards the truth?
Decius, go tell them Caesar will not come.

DECIUS   Most mighty Caesar, let me know some cause,
Lest I be laughed at when I tell them so.   70

CAESAR   The cause is in my will: I will not come.
That is enough to satisfy the Senate;
But for your private satisfaction,
Because I love you, I will let you know.
Calpurnia here, my wife, stays me at home.   75
She dreamt to-night she saw my statue,
Which, like a fountain with an hundred spouts,
Did run pure blood; and many lusty Romans
Came smiling and did bathe their hands in it.
And these does she apply for warnings and portents   80
And evils imminent, and on her knee
Hath begged that I will stay at home to-day.

DECIUS   This dream is all amiss interpreted;
It was a vision fair and fortunate.
Your statue spouting blood in many pipes,   85
In which so many smiling Romans bathed,
Signifies that from you great Rome shall suck
Reviving blood, and that great men shall press
For tinctures, stains, relics, and cognizance.
This by Calpurnia's dream is signified.   90

CAESAR   And this way have you well expounded it.

DECIUS   I have, when you have heard what I can say;
And know it now. The Senate have concluded
To give this day a crown to mighty Caesar.
If you shall send them word you will not come,   95
Their minds may change. Besides, it were a mock
Apt to be rendered, for some one to say
'Break up the Senate till another time,
When Caesar's wife shall meet with better dreams.'
If Caesar hide himself, shall they not whisper   100
'Lo. Caesar is afraid?'
Pardon me, Caesar; for my dear dear love
To your proceeding bids me tell you this,
And reason to my love is liable.

| CAESAR | Shall I lie about this? Have I conquered so much territory that I am afraid to tell old men the truth? Decius, tell the senators that Caesar will not come. |

| DECIUS | Mighty Caesar, give me some reason. I don't want the senators to laugh at your message. |

| CAESAR | My reason is in my will: I will not come. That is all the Senate needs to know. But to satisfy your concern and because you are my friend, I will tell you the real reason. My wife Calpurnia wants me to stay home. Last night, she dreamed about my statue, which she saw pouring blood from a hundred spouts. Eager, smiling Romans approached the statue to bathe their hands in the flow. She takes this dream as a warning of some approaching evil. She has begged on her knees that I stay home today. |

| DECIUS | You have misinterpreted the dream. It was a positive vision. The flow of blood from your statue from many openings signifies a life-giving force that nurtures the smiling citizens of Rome. From this blood great men shall seek souvenirs and blessing. This is what Calpurnia's dream signifies. |

| CAESAR | You have done a good job of explaining the dream. |

| DECIUS | I am sure that what I have to say will support my interpretation. Today, the Senate intends to crown you king. If you send a message that you are staying home, they will change their minds about the crown. Another possibility is mockery from someone saying, "Cancel the Senate until Caesar's wife has less frightening dreams." If you hide at home, will they not whisper, "Caesar is afraid"? Pardon me, Caesar, for being blunt. My affection for you forces me to be honest. |

CAESAR	How foolish do your fears seem now, Calpurnia! 105
	I am ashamed I did yield to them.
	Give me my robe, for I will go.
	[Enter BRUTUS, LIGARIUS, METELLUS, CASCA,
	TREBONIUS, CINNA, and PUBLIUS]
	And look where Publius is come to fetch me.
PUBLIUS	Good morrow, Caesar.
CAESAR	Welcome, Publius.
	What, Brutus, are you stirred so early too? 110
	Good morrow, Casca. Caius Ligarius,
	Caesar was ne'er so much your enemy
	As that same ague which hath made you lean.
	What is't o'clock?
BRUTUS	Caesar, 'tis strucken eight.
CAESAR	I thank you for your pains and courtesy. 115
	[Enter ANTONY]
	See! Antony, that revels long a-nights,
	Is notwithstanding up. Good morrow, Antony.
ANTONY	So to most noble Caesar.
CAESAR	Bid them prepare within.
	I am to blame to be thus waited for.
	Now, Cinna. Now, Metellus. What, Trebonius; 120
	I have an hour's talk in store for you;
	Remember that you call on me to-day;
	Be near me, that I may remember you.
TREBONIUS	Caesar, I will *[Aside]* And so near will I be
	That your best friends shall wish I had been further. 125
CAESAR	Good friends, go in and taste some wine with me
	And we (like friends) will straightway go together.
BRUTUS	*[Aside]* That every like is not the same. O Caesar
	The heart of Brutus erns to think upon.
	[Exeunt]

CAESAR	Your jitters seem foolish, Calpurnia! I am ashamed that I listened to your fears. Hand me my toga. I am going to the Senate. *[Enter BRUTUS, LIGARIUS, METELLUS, CASCA, TREBONIUS, CINNA, and PUBLIUS]* Look, Publius is here to escort me.
PUBLIUS	Good morning, Caesar.
CAESAR	Welcome, Publius. Brutus, why are you out so early this morning? Good morning, Casca. Caius Ligarius, I was never as tough on you as the illness that has made you thin. What time is it?
BRUTUS	Caesar, it is 8:00 a.m.
CAESAR	I am grateful for your attention and courtesy to me. *[ANTONY enters]* Look! Antony, who carouses late at night, is already up. Good morning, Antony.
ANTONY	The same to you, sir.
CAESAR	Tell my staff to prepare to leave. It is my fault for keeping them waiting. Let's go, Cinna, Metellus. You, too, Trebonius. I need an hour with you. Remember to seek me out today. Stay close by to remind me that I need to speak to you.
TREBONIUS	Yes, Caesar. *[To himself]* I will be so close that your best friends will regret it.
CAESAR	Come, friends, and share some wine with me. As friends, we will leave the house together.
BRUTUS	*[To himself]* Not every relationship is the same. Oh Caesar, I grieve to think about conspiracy. *[Brutus goes out]*

ACT II

ACT II, SCENE 3

A street.

[Enter ARTEMIDORUS, reading a paper]

ARTEMIDORUS 'Caesar, beware of Brutus; take heed
of Cassius; come not near Casca; have an eye to
Cinna; trust not Trebonius; mark well Metellus
Cimber; Decius Brutus loves thee not; thou hast
wronged Caius Ligarius. There is but one mind in   5
all these men, and it is bent against Caesar. If thou
beest not immortal, look about you. Security gives
way to conspiracy. The mighty gods defend thee!
               Thy lover,
                  Artemidorus.'   10
Here will I stand till Caesar pass along
And as a suitor will I give him this.
My heart laments that virtue cannot live
Out of the teeth of emulation.
If thou read this, O Caesar, thou mayest live;   15
If not, the Fates with traitors do contrive. *[Exit]*

ORIGINAL

ACT II, SCENE 3

A street.

[Enter ARTEMIDORUS, reading a note]

ARTEMIDORUS   "Caesar, beware of Brutus and Cassius. Avoid Casca. Keep
your eye on Cinna. Don't trust Trebonius. Watch out for
Metellus Cimber. Decius Brutus is your enemy. You have
wronged Caius Ligarius. These men have one intention—to
harm Caesar. If you are mortal, notice what is happening
around you. If you are too lax, you allow conspiracy to
grow. The gods defend you!

> Your friend,
> Artemidorus."

I will stand here until Caesar passes by and, as a petitioner,
I will hand him this personal note. I regret that goodness
cannot survive free of envy. If you read this note, Caesar,
you may survive. If you don't read it, destiny will favor
traitors. *[He departs]*

ACT II, SCENE 4

Before Brutus' house.

[Enter PORTIA and LUCIUS]

PORTIA	I prithee, boy, run to the Senate House.
	Stay not to answer me, but get thee gone!
	Why dost thou stay?
LUCIUS	To know my errand, madam.
PORTIA	I would have had thee there and here again
	Ere I can tell thee what thou shouldst do there. 5
	[Aside] O constancy, be strong upon my side,
	Set a huge mountain 'tween my heart and tongue!
	I have a man's mind, but a woman's might.
	How hard it is for women to keep counsel!
	Art thou here yet?
LUCIUS	Madam, what should I do? 10
	Run to the Capitol and nothing else?
PORTIA	Yes, bring me word, boy, if thy lord look well,
	For he went sickly forth; and take good note
	What Caesar doth, what suitors press to him.
	Hark, boy! What noise is that? 15
LUCIUS	I hear none, madam.
PORTIA	Prithee listen well.
	I heard a bustling rumour like a fray,
	And the wind brings it from the Capitol.
LUCIUS	Sooth, madam, I hear nothing.
	[Enter the Soothsayer]
PORTIA	Come hither, fellow. Which way hast thou been? 20
SOOTHSAYER	At mine own house, good lady.
PORTIA	What is't o'clock?
SOOTHSAYER	About the ninth hour, lady.
PORTIA	Is Caesar yet gone to the Capitol?
SOOTHSAYER	Madam, not yet. I go take my stand,
	To see him pass on to the Capitol. 25
PORTIA	Thou hast some suit to Caesar, hast thou not?

ACT II, SCENE 4

Before Brutus' house.

[Enter PORTIA and LUCIUS]

PORTIA   Please, boy, run to the Senate House. Don't stand there, get going! Why aren't you moving?

LUCIUS   What is my errand, madam?

PORTIA   You could be there and back before I could explain your errand. *[To herself]* Oh self-control, help me. Set a huge mountain between my wishes and my words! I have a man's intellect, but a woman's strength. It is difficult for women to keep secrets! Haven't you gone yet?

LUCIUS   Madam, what is my mission? Run to the Capitol and nothing else?

PORTIA   Bring me a report on Brutus' health. He was sick when he left home. Notice Caesar's actions and what petitioners seek his attention. Listen, boy! What is that noise?

LUCIUS   I don't hear anything, madam.

PORTIA   Please listen carefully. I hear a bustle like a fight. The wind directs the sound from the Capitol.

LUCIUS   Truly, madam, I don't hear anything. *[The fortune teller enters]*

PORTIA   Come here, sir. From what direction did you come?

SOOTHSAYER From my house, lady.

PORTIA   What time is it?

SOOTHSAYER About 9:00 a.m., lady.

PORTIA   Has Caesar left for the Capitol?

SOOTHSAYER Not yet, madam. I am going to stand here while he walks by to the Capitol.

PORTIA   You have a petition for Caesar, don't you?

TRANSLATION

ACT II

SOOTHSAYER	That I have, lady, if it will please Caesar
	To be so good to Caesar as to hear me:
	I shall beseech him to befriend himself.
PORTIA	Why, know'st thou any harm's intended towards him? 30
SOOTHSAYER	None that I know will be, much that I fear may chance.
	Good morrow to you. Here the street is narrow.
	The throng that follows Caesar at the heels,
	Of senators, of praetors, common suitors,
	Will crowd a feeble man almost to death. 35
	I'll get me to a place more void and there
	Speak to great Caesar as he comes along. *[Exit]*
PORTIA	I must go in. Ay me, how weak a thing
	The heart of woman is! O Brutus,
	The heavens speed thee in thine enterprise! 40
	Sure the boy heard me.—Brutus hath a suit
	That Caesar will not grant.—O, I grow faint.—
	Run, Lucius, and commend me to my lord;
	Say I am merry. Come to me again
	And bring me word what he doth say to thee. 45
	[Exeunt severally]

SOOTHSAYER	I have, lady. If Caesar will accept a personal message, I will beg him to watch out for his own safety.
PORTIA	Do you know of any plot against him?
SOOTHSAYER	I know nothing for certain, but I fear something may happen. Good day. The street is narrow here. Caesar's throng of senators, magistrates, and ordinary petitioners could trample a weak man. I will choose an empty spot and greet Caesar as he walks by. *[He goes out]*
PORTIA	I must return to the house. A woman's emotions are so weak. Oh Brutus, God go with you on this mission! I'm afraid that Lucius heard what I said. Brutus has a petition that Caesar rejects. Oh, I feel faint. Run, Lucius, and carry my good wishes to my husband. Return to me with news from Brutus. *[They depart in different directions]*

ACT II

ACT III, SCENE 1

Rome, before the Capitol.

[Flourish. Enter CAESAR, BRUTUS, CASSIUS, CASCA, DECIUS, METELLUS, TREBONIUS, CINNA, ANTONY, LEPIDUS, ARTEMIDORUS, POPILIUS, PUBLIUS, and the Soothsayer]

CAESAR	The ides of March are come.
SOOTHSAYER	Ay, Caesar, but not gone.
ARTEMIDORUS	Hail, Caesar! Read this schedule.
DECIUS	Trebonius doth desire you to o'erread (At your best leisure) this his humble suit.
ARTEMIDORUS	O Caesar, read mine first, for mine's a suit That touches Caesar nearer. Read it, great Caesar!
CAESAR	What touches us ourself shall be last served.
ARTEMIDORUS	Delay not, Caesar! Read it instantly!
CAESAR	What, is the fellow mad?
PUBLIUS	Sirrah, give place.
CASSIUS	What, urge you your petitions in the street? Come to the Capitol. *[CAESAR goes to the Capitol, the rest following]*
POPILIUS	I wish your enterprise to-day may thrive.
CASSIUS	What enterprise, Popilius?
POPILIUS	Fare you well. *[Advances to CAESAR]*
BRUTUS	What said Popilius Lena?
CASSIUS	He wished to-day our enterprise might thrive. I fear our purpose is discovered.
BRUTUS	Look how he makes to Caesar. Mark him.
CASSIUS	Casca, be sudden, for we fear prevention. Brutus, what shall be done? If this be known, Cassius or Caesar never shall turn back, For I will slay myself.
BRUTUS	Cassius, be constant. Popilius Lena speaks not of our purposes; For look, he smiles, and Caesar doth not change.

5

10

15

20

ORIGINAL

ACT III, SCENE 1

Rome, before the Capitol.

[A trumpet fanfare. Entering are CAESAR, BRUTUS, CASSIUS, CASCA, DECIUS, METELLUS, TREBONIUS, CINNA, ANTONY, LEPIDUS, ARTEMIDORUS, POPILIUS, PUBLIUS, and a fortune teller]

CAESAR	It is March 15.
SOOTHSAYER	Yes, Caesar, but the day is not over.
ARTEMIDORUS	Greetings, Caesar! Read this message.
DECIUS	Trebonius wants you to scan his petition when you have time.
ARTEMIDORUS	Oh Caesar, read mine first. The note concerns you personally. Please read it, Caesar!
CAESAR	I will attend to personal matters after I have heard these other petitions.
ARTEMIDORUS	Don't delay, Caesar! Read it immediately!
CAESAR	Are you crazy?
PUBLIUS	Sir, get out of the way.
CASSIUS	Are you pressing your petition in the street? Bring it to the Capitol. *[CAESAR goes to the Capitol, the rest following]*
POPILIUS	I wish your plan may go well today.
CASSIUS	What plan, Popilius?
POPILIUS	Farewell. *[He walks up to CAESAR]*
BRUTUS	What did Popilius Lena say?
CASSIUS	He hoped our plan might succeed today. I'm afraid our conspiracy is no longer a secret.
BRUTUS	Look how he fawns on Caesar. Watch Popilius.
CASSIUS	Casca, be quick, lest we be stopped. Brutus, what shall we do? If our conspiracy is public knowledge, neither I nor Caesar will survive, for I will kill myself.
BRUTUS	Steady, Cassius. Popilius Lena is not referring to the conspiracy. See—he smiles at Caesar and Caesar shows no concern.

TRANSLATION

CASSIUS	Trebonius knows his time, for look you, Brutus, 25 He draws Mark Antony out of the way. *[Exeunt ANTONY and TREBONIUS]*
DECIUS	Where is Metellus Cimber? Let him go And presently prefer his suit to Caesar.
BRUTUS	He is addressed. Press near and second him.
CINNA	Casca, you are the first that rears your hand. 30
CAESAR	Are we all ready? What is now amiss That Caesar and his Senate must redress?
METELLUS	Most high, most mighty, and most puissant Caesar, Metellus Cimber throws before thy seat An humble heart. *[Kneels]*
CAESAR	I must prevent thee, Cimber. 35 These couchings, and these lowly courtesies Might fire the blood of ordinary men And turn preordinance and first decree Into the lane of children. Be not fond To think that Caesar bears such rebel blood 40 That will be thawed from the true quality With that which melteth fools—I mean sweet words, Low-crooked curtsies, and base spaniel fawning. Thy brother by decree is banished. If thou dost bend and pray and fawn for him, 45 I spurn thee like a cur out of my way. Know, Caesar doth not wrong, nor without cause Will he be satisfied.
METELLUS	Is there no voice more worthy than my own, To sound more sweetly in great Caesar's ear 50 For the repealing of my banished brother?
BRUTUS	I kiss thy hand, but not in flattery, Caesar, Desiring thee that Publius Cimber may Have an immediate freedom of repeal.
CAESAR	What, Brutus?
CASSIUS	Pardon, Caesar! Caesar, pardon! 55 As low as to thy foot doth Cassius fall To beg enfranchisement for Publius Cimber.

CASSIUS	Trebonius is right on time. Look, Brutus, he draws Mark Antony out of the way. *[ANTONY and TREBONIUS depart]*
DECIUS	Where is Metellus Cimber? Have him offer his petition to Caesar immediately.
BRUTUS	He is ready. Come closer and support his request.
CINNA	Casca, you are the first to raise your weapon.
CAESAR	Are we all ready? What issue are Caesar and the Senate considering?
METELLUS	Most honored, most mighty, and most powerful Caesar, I bring you a humble heart. *[METELLUS kneels]*
CAESAR	Get up, Metellus Cimber. Such groveling and excessive courtesy might stir an ordinary leader and earn you preferential treatment. Don't assume that I will fall for that trick. I detest sugary words, low bows, and dog-like currying of favor. Your brother is in exile. If you are bowing and begging and groveling on his behalf, I will kick you out of my way like a dog. I make no faulty decisions and I don't change my edicts without good reason.

ACT III

METELLUS	Is there no one who can gain Caesar's promise to return my brother from exile?
BRUTUS	I kiss your hand, Caesar, but not to flatter you. I beg you to repeal the banishment of Publius Cimber.
CAESAR	What, Brutus?
CASSIUS	Allow me, Caesar, to bow to your foot and beg reinstatement for Publius Cimber.

TRANSLATION

CAESAR	I could be well moved, if I were as you; If I could pray to move, prayers would move me: But I am constant as the Northern Star, 60 Of whose true-fixed and resting quality There is no fellow in the firmament. The skies are painted with unnumber'd sparks, They are all fire, and every one doth shine; But there's but one in all doth hold his place. 65 So in the world: 'tis furnished well with men, And men are flesh and blood, and apprehensive; Yet in the number I do know but one That unassailable holds on his rank, Unshaked of motion; and that I am he, 70 Let me a little show it, even in this— That I was constant Cimber should be banished And constant do remain to keep him so.
CINNA	O Caesar.
CAESAR	Hence! Wilt thou lift up Olympus?
DECIUS	Great Caesar.
CAESAR	Doth not Brutus bootless kneel? 75
CASCA	Speak hands for me. *[They stab CAESAR—CASCA first, BRUTUS last]*
CAESAR	*Et tu, Brute?*—Then fall Caesar. *[Dies]*
CINNA	Liberty! Freedom! Tyranny is dead! Run hence, proclaim, cry it about the streets!
CASSIUS	Some to the common pulpits and cry out 80 'Liberty, freedom, and enfranchisement!'
BRUTUS	People and senators, be not affrighted. Fly not; stand still. Ambition's debt is paid.
CASCA	Go to the pulpit, Brutus.
DECIUS	And Cassius too.
BRUTUS	Where's Publius? 85
CINNA	Here, quite confounded with the mutiny.
METELLUS	Stand fast together, lest some friend of Caesar's Should chance—

CAESAR	If I were you, Cassius, I might change my mind. I might let entreaties persuade me. But I am as unchanging as Polaris, the North Star, which is more dependable and unchanging than any other heavenly body. Countless stars twinkle in the sky. They all shine like fire. But there is one that stays in place. It is the same with the world. There are plenty of people. Humans are mortal and reasonable. But I know of only one who refuses to give in to pleas. That person is me. Let me display my constancy. I agreed that Cimber should be banished. My decree has not changed.
CINNA	Oh Caesar.
CAESAR	Go away. Would you move a mountain?
DECIUS	Great Caesar.
CAESAR	Didn't Brutus fail to change my mind?
CASCA	Let my hands speak for me. *[The conspirators stab CAESAR. CASCA begins the assassination. BRUTUS ends it]*
CAESAR	Even you, Brutus? Then Caesar must fall. *[He dies]*
CINNA	Liberty! Freedom! The tyrant is dead! Run outside and proclaim the news in the streets!
CASSIUS	Some of you, go to the speaker's platforms and proclaim, "Liberty, freedom, and citizen's rights."
BRUTUS	People and senators, don't be afraid. Don't run away. Stay here. The ambitious man is dead.
CASCA	Go to the public lectern, Brutus.
DECIUS	Cassius, go with Brutus.
BRUTUS	Where's Publius?
CINNA	Here he is, completely astounded at this assassination.
METELLUS	Stay in a tight group lest some of Caesar's friends should happen to—

ACT III

TRANSLATION

BRUTUS	Talk not of standing! Publius, good cheer.
	There is no harm intended to your person 90
	Nor to no Roman else. So tell them, Publius.

CASSIUS	And leave us, Publius, lest that the people,
	Rushing on us, should do your age some mischief.

BRUTUS	Do so; and let no man abide this deed
	But we the doers.
	[Enter TREBONIUS]

CASSIUS	Where is Antony? 95

TREBONIUS	Fled to his house amazed.
	Men, wives, and children, stare, cry out, and run,
	As it were doomsday.

BRUTUS	Fates, we will know your pleasures.
	That we shall die, we know; 'tis but the time,
	And drawing days out, that men stand upon. 100

CASCA	Why, he that cuts off twenty years of life
	Cuts off so many years of fearing death.

BRUTUS	Grant that, and then is death a benefit.
	So are we Caesar's friends, that have abridged
	His time of fearing death. Stoop, Romans, stoop, 105
	And let us bathe our hands in Caesar's blood
	Up to the elbows and besmear our swords.
	Then walk we forth, even to the market place,
	And waving our red weapons o'er our heads,
	Let's all cry 'Peace, freedom and liberty!' 110

CASSIUS	Stoop then and wash. How many ages hence
	Shall this our lofty scene be acted over
	In states unborn and accents yet unknown!

BRUTUS	How many times shall Caesar bleed in sport,
	That now on Pompey's basis lies along 115
	No worthier than the dust!

CASSIUS	So oft as that shall be,
	So often shall the knot of us be called
	The men that gave their country liberty.

DECIUS	What, shall we forth?

CASSIUS	Ay, every man away.
	Brutus shall lead, and we will grace his heels 120
	With the most boldest and best hearts of Rome.
	[Enter a Servant]

ORIGINAL

BRUTUS	Don't stand here! Publius, be glad. No one will harm you or any other Roman. Tell everybody, Publius.
CASSIUS	Leave the conspirators, Publius, lest onlookers should harm an old man.
BRUTUS	Do as he says, Publius. And let no one claim this deed except the conspirators. *[Enter TREBONIUS]*
CASSIUS	Where is Antony?
TREBONIUS	He ran terrified to his house. Men, women, and children gape, cry, and run as if it were the end of the world.
BRUTUS	We all know that destiny will end our lives, but people worry about when they will die.
CASCA	A man who dies 20 years too soon saves himself 20 years of fearing death.
BRUTUS	I agree. As Caesar's friends, we have shortened the time that he might have feared dying. Kneel, Romans, and rinse your hands in Caesar's blood to the elbows and smear your swords. Let's walk out the door and go to the market waving these bloody swords over our heads and proclaiming "Peace, freedom, and liberty!"
CASSIUS	Kneel and wash your hands. People will re-enact this scene for years in countries and languages that don't exist yet.
BRUTUS	How many times will Caesar's death be acted out on the stage!
CASSIUS	Whenever the play is performed, we will be called libera-tors of Rome.
DECIUS	Shall we go outside?
CASSIUS	Yes, all of us. Brutus will lead the way. We will follow like Rome's most daring and greathearted citizens. *[Enter a Servant]*

ACT III

TRANSLATION

BRUTUS   Soft! who comes here? A friend of Antony's.

SERVANT   Thus, Brutus, did my master bid me kneel;
Thus did Mark Antony bid me fall down;
And being prostrate, thus he bade me say;   125
Brutus is noble, wise, valiant, and honest;
Caesar was mighty, bold, royal, and loving.
Say I love Brutus and I honour him;
Say I feared Caesar, honoured him, and loved him.
If Brutus will vouchsafe that Antony   130
May safely come to him and be resolved
How Caesar hath deserved to lie in death,
Mark Antony shall not love Caesar dead
So well as Brutus living; but will follow
The fortunes and affairs of noble Brutus   135
Thorough the hazards of this untrod state
With all true faith. So, says my master Antony.

BRUTUS   Thy master is a wise and valiant Roman.
I never thought him worse.
Tell him, so please him come unto this place,   140
He shall be satisfied and, by my honour,
Depart untouched.

SERVANT   I'll fetch him presently. *[Exit]*

BRUTUS   I know that we shall have him well to friend.

CASSIUS   I wish we may. But yet I have a mind
That fears him much; and my misgiving still   145
Falls shrewdly to the purpose.
[Enter ANTONY]

BRUTUS   But here comes Antony. Welcome, Mark Antony.

BRUTUS	Wait. Who is coming? Is this Antony's friend?
SERVANT	Brutus, my master sent me to kneel, fall on my face, and say this: Brutus is respectable, wise, brave, and honest; Caesar was mighty, daring, kingly, and generous. Tell the conspirators that I admire and respect Brutus; tell the conspirators that I revered, honored, and loved Caesar. If Brutus will promise that Antony may safely come and question why Caesar deserved assassination, Mark Antony will honor the conspirators more than he honors the dead friend. Antony will engage Brutus in discussion, even though the outcome of this killing is uncertain. This is my message from my master, Antony.
BRUTUS	Your master is a wise and brave Roman. I never thought otherwise about him. Tell him to join us here. I promise to answer his questions and leave him unharmed.
SERVANT	I will get him immediately. *[He goes out]*
BRUTUS	I believe that we are right to befriend Antony.
CASSIUS	I hope you are right. But I have misgivings about him that may prove true. *[Enter ANTONY]*
BRUTUS	Here comes Antony. Welcome, Mark Antony.

ACT III

ANTONY

O mighty Caesar! dost thou lie so low?
Are all the conquests, glories, triumphs, spoils,
Shrunk to this little measure? Fare thee well. 150
I know not gentlemen, what you intend,
Who else must be let blood, who else is rank.
If I myself, there is no hour so fit
As Caesar's death's hour; nor no instrument
Of half that worth as those your swords, made rich 155
With the most noble blood of all this world.
I do beseech ye, if you bear me hard,
Now, whilst your purpled hands do reek and smoke
Fulfil your pleasure. Live a thousand years,
I shall not find myself so apt to die; 160
No place will please me so, no mean of death,
As here by Caesar, and by you cut off,
The choice and master spirits of this age.

BRUTUS

O Antony, beg not your death of us!
Though now we must appear bloody and cruel, 165
As by our hands and this our present act
You see we do, yet see you but our hands
And this the bleeding business they have done.
Our hearts you see not. They are pitiful;
And pity to the general wrong of Rome 170
(As fire drives out fire, so pity pity)
Hath done this deed on Caesar. For your part,
To you our swords have leaden points, Mark Antony.
Our arms in strength of malice, and our hearts
Of brothers' temper do receive you in 175
With all kind love, good thoughts, and reverence.

CASSIUS

Your voice shall be as strong as any man's
In the disposing of new dignities.

BRUTUS

Only be patient till we have appeased
The multitude, beside themselves with fear, 180
And then we will deliver you the cause
Why I, that did love Caesar when I struck him,
Have thus proceeded.

ANTONY	Oh great Caesar! Have you fallen so far? Are all your victories, glory, parades, and treasure shrunk to this terrible death. Farewell. I don't know what you gentlemen plan to do, who else you plan to kill, who else must die. If you plan to kill me, I would be honored to die along with Caesar. There is no death weapon so worthy as the swords that drip Caesar's blood. I beg you, if you consider me an enemy, carry out your intent while your hands are still bloody. If I should live a thousand years, I will never find myself more ready to die. No place nor weapon is more suitable than that which served Caesar's assassination.
BRUTUS	Oh Antony, don't ask us to kill you! Although we appear savage and cruel for our bloody hands and this corpse, you look only at the hands that have killed a tyrant. You can't see our hearts. They pity Rome, for whose benefit we had no pity on Caesar. As for you, our swords are blunt, Mark Antony. These arms that killed Caesar receive you as a brother with our affection, good intentions, and respect.
CASSIUS	You will have a central part in the restructuring of the government.
BRUTUS	Please wait until we have quieted citizens and eased their fears. We will offer you an explanation of why I stabbed a man whom I loved.

ACT III

ANTONY   I doubt not of your wisdom.
Let each man render me his bloody hand.
First, Marcus Brutus, will I shake with you;   185
Next, Caius Cassius, do I take your hand;
Now, Decius Brutus, yours; now yours, Metellus;
Yours, Cinna; and, my valiant Casca, yours.
Though last, not least in love, yours, good Trebonius.
Gentlemen all—Alas, what shall I say?   190
My credit now stands on such slippery ground
That one of two bad ways you must conceit me,
Either a coward or a flatterer.
That I did love thee, Caesar, O, 'tis true!
If then thy spirit look upon us now,   195
Shall it not grieve thee dearer than thy death
To see thy Antony making his peace,
Shaking the bloody fingers of thy foes,
Most noble! in the presence of thy corse?
Had I as many eyes as thou hast wounds,   200
Weeping as fast as they stream forth thy blood,
It would become me better than to close
In terms of friendship with thine enemies.
Pardon me, Julius! Here wast thou bayed, brave hart;
Here didst thou fall; and here thy hunters stand,   205
Signed in thy spoil, and crimsoned in thy lethe.
O world, thou wast the forest to this hart;
And this indeed, O world, the heart of thee!
How like a deer, stroken by many princes,
Dost thou here lie!   210

CASSIUS   Mark Antony—

ANTONY   Pardon me, Caius Cassius.
The enemies of Caesar shall say this:
Then, in a friend, it is cold modesty.

CASSIUS   I blame you not for praising Caesar so;
But what compact mean you to have with us?   215
Will you be pricked in number of our friends,
Or shall we on, and not depend on you?

ANTONY   Therefore I took your hands, but was indeed
Swayed from the point by looking down on Caesar.
Friends am I with you all, and love you all,   220
Upon this hope, that you shall give me reasons
Why and wherein Caesar was dangerous.

ORIGINAL

ANTONY	I trust your wisdom. Let me shake your bloody hands. First, I shake hands with Marcus Brutus, then Caius Cassius. Then Decius Brutus, Metellus, Cinna, brave Casca, and finally, yours, Trebonius. Gentlemen, what can I add? My position is so uncertain that you must view me as either a coward or a sell-out. I did love you, Caesar. If your spirit is looking on us, are you disappointed to see me make peace with your bloody-handed killers? In sight of your corpse? If I had as many eyes as you have stab wounds poring tears as rapidly as you leak blood, it would be to my advantage to make friends with your killers. Paron me, Julius! This is where you were cornered, brave deer. Here is where you died and here your killers stand stained with your blood. Oh world, you belonged to Caesar. He was the heart of the world. Like a deer, struck by many pursuers, you lie here!

CASSIUS	Mark Antony—
ANTONY	Excuse me, Caius Cassius. Caesar's enemies shall describe my grief as moderate.
CASSIUS	I don't blame you for praising Caesar. But what agreement do you want with us? Are you one of the conspirators, or should we move on and leave you out?
ANTONY	I shook hands for a reason, but my attention strayed from you to Caesar's body. I am your friend and admire you all. I hope that you will justify why Caesar deserved to be killed.

TRANSLATION

BRUTUS	Or else were this a savage spectacle.
	Our reasons are so full of good regard
	There were you, Antony, the son of Caesar, 225
	You should be satisfied.
ANTONY	That's all I seek;
	And am moreover suitor that I may
	Produce his body to the market place
	And in the pulpit, as becomes a friend,
	Speak in the order of his funeral. 230
BRUTUS	You shall, Mark Antony.
CASSIUS	Brutus, a word with you.
	[Aside to BRUTUS]
	You know not what you do. Do not consent
	That Antony speak in his funeral.
	Know you how much the people may be moved
	By that which he will utter?
BRUTUS	*[Aside to CASSIUS]* By your pardon— 235
	I will myself into the pulpit first
	And show the reasons for our Caesar's death.
	What Antony shall speak, I will protest
	He speaks by leave and by permission;
	And that we are contented Caesar shall 240
	Have all true rites and lawful ceremonies.
	It shall advantage more than do us wrong.
CASSIUS	*[Aside to BRUTUS]* I know not what may fall. I like it not.
BRUTUS	Mark Antony, here, take you Caesar's body
	You shall not in your funeral speech blame us, 245
	But speak all good you can devise of Caesar;
	And say you do't by our permission.
	Else shall you not have any hand at all
	About his funeral. And you shall speak
	In the same pulpit whereto I am going, 250
	After my speech is ended.
ANTONY	Be it so.
	I do desire no more.
BRUTUS	Prepare the body then, and follow us.
	[Exeunt all except ANTONY]

BRUTUS	Otherwise, this would be a barbarous assassination. Our reasons were so sound that, even if you were Caesar's son, you would agree with us.
ANTONY	Justification is all I ask. I also want to carry his body to the market and stand at the public lectern like a friend to speak at his funeral.
BRUTUS	You may, Mark Antony.
CASSIUS	Brutus, may I have a private word with you? *[In private to BRUTUS]* You don't know what you are agreeing to. Don't allow Antony to speak at the funeral. Don't you think that he might move the people with his words?
BRUTUS	*[In private to CASSIUS]* With your permission, I will speak first to the people and justify the assassination. I will explain that Antony may speak with the permission of the conspirators. It will benefit us to assure Caesar an appropriate ritual and a state funeral.
CASSIUS	*[In private to BRUTUS]* I don't trust the outcome. I don't like this plan.
BRUTUS	Mark Antony, take up Caesar's body. In your funeral address, you may not blame us. Rather, say good things about Caesar. Tell the people that we are allowing you to speak. Otherwise, you will have no part in his funeral. You may speak at the same lectern after I finish.
ANTONY	I agree. I don't want anything else.
BRUTUS	Make the body ready and follow us. *[Everyone leaves except ANTONY]*

ACT III

ANTONY	O, pardon me, thou bleeding piece of earth,
	That I am meek and gentle with these butchers! 255
	Thou art the ruins of the noblest man
	That ever lived in the tide of times.
	Woe to the hand that shed this costly blood!
	Over thy wounds now do I prophesy
	(Which, like dumb mouths, do ope their ruby lips 260
	To beg the voice and utterance of my tongue),
	A curse shall light upon the limbs of men;
	Domestic fury and fierce civil strife
	Shall cumber all the parts of Italy;
	Blood and destruction shall be so in use 265
	And dreadful objects so familiar
	That mothers shall but smile when they behold
	Their infants quartered with the hands of war,
	All pity choked with custom of fell deeds
	And Caesar's spirit, ranging for revenge, 270
	With Ate by his side come hot from hell,
	Shall in these confines with a monarch's voice
	Cry 'Havoc!' and let slip the dogs of war,
	That this foul deed shall smell above the earth
	With carrion men, groaning for burial. 275
	[Enter OCTAVIUS' servant]
	You serve Octavius Caesar, do you not?
SERVANT	I do, Mark Antony.
ANTONY	Caesar did write for him to come to Rome.
SERVANT	He did receive his letters and is coming,
	And bid me say to you by word of mouth— 280
	O Caesar!
ANTONY	Thy heart is big. Get thee apart and weep.
	Passion, I see, is catching; for mine eyes,
	Seeing those beads of sorrow stand in thine,
	Began to water. Is thy master coming? 285
SERVANT	He lies to-night within seven leagues of Rome.

ANTONY	Oh pardon me, my bloody friend, that I show no hostility to these butchers! You are the remains of the noblest man who ever lived. I curse the hand that stabbed you! I predict over your wounds (which look like red mouths that depend on me to speak for them): Romans shall incur rebellion and civil war that will spread over Italy. Slaughter and mayhem will be so common and weapons so visible that mothers will only smile when warriors chop their babies apart. Pity will disappear as murder becomes customary. Caesar's spirit will roam about in search of revenge. Accompanied by Ate, the goddess of destruction risen from hell, Caesar will proclaim catastrophe and let chaos run free. This foul assassination shall smell even more foul from the rotting carcasses waiting for burial. *[Enter OCTAVIUS' servant]* You are the servant of Octavius Caesar, aren't you?

ACT III

SERVANT	I am, Mark Antony.
ANTONY	Caesar sent a message summoning Octavius to Rome.
SERVANT	He received the message and is coming. He asked me to tell you—Oh Caesar!
ANTONY	You have a great heart. Weep in private. Emotion spreads easily. My eyes, seeing your tears, began to cry. Is Octavius coming?
SERVANT	By tonight, he will be only 7 hours' travel from Rome.

TRANSLATION

ANTONY   Post back with speed and tell him what hath chanced.
              Here is a mourning Rome, a dangerous Rome,
              No Rome of safety for Octavius yet.
              Hie hence and tell him so. Yet stay awhile.   290
              Thou shalt not back till I have born this corse
              Into the market place. There shall I try
              In my oration how the people take
              The cruel issue of these bloody men;
              According to the which thou shalt discourse   295
              To young Octavius of the state of things.
              Lend me your hand. *[Exeunt with CAESAR'S body]*

ANTONY   Hurry back and tell him what has happened. Rome is sorrowful and unsettled. It is unsafe for Octavius to be here. Hurry to him and tell him. But remain for a while. Don't return to Octavius until I have carried the corpse into the market. There I will learn from my speech how Romans are responding to the assassination. Then you can relay the information to Octavius. Help me carry him. *[They depart with CAESAR's body]*

ACT III, SCENE 2

The Forum.

[Enter BRUTUS and goes into the pulpit, and CASSIUS and the citizens]

CITIZENS	We will be satisfied! Let us be satisfied!
BRUTUS	Then follow me and give me audience, friends.
	Cassius, go you into the other street
	And part the numbers.
	Those that will hear me speak, let 'em stay here; 5
	Those that will follow Cassius, go with him;
	And public reasons shall be rendered
	Of Caesar's death.
1ST CITIZEN	I will hear Brutus speak.
2ND CITIZEN	I will hear Cassius, and compare their reasons
	When severally we hear them rendered. 10
3RD CITIZEN	The noble Brutus is ascended. Silence!
BRUTUS	Be patient till the last.

Romans, countrymen, and lovers, hear me for my
cause, and be silent, that you may hear. Believe
me for mine honour, and have respect to mine   15
honour, that you may believe. Censure me in your
wisdom and awake your senses, that you may the
better judge. If there be any in this assembly, any
dear friend of Caesar's, to him I say that Brutus'
love to Caesar was no less than his. If then that   20
friend demand why Brutus rose against Caesar,
this is my answer: Not that I loved Caesar less,
but that I loved Rome more. Had you rather Caesar
were living, and die all slaves, than that Caesar
were dead, to live all freemen? As Caesar loved   25
me, I weep for him; as he was fortunate, I rejoice
at it; as he was valiant, I honour him; but—
as he was ambitious, I slew him. There is tears for
his love; joy for his fortune; honour for his valour;
and death for his ambition. Who is here so base that 30
would be a bondman? If any, speak; for him I have
offended. Who is here so rude that would not be a
Roman? If any, speak; for him have I offended.
Who is here so vile that will not love his country? If
any, speak; for him I have offended. I pause for a   35
reply.

ACT III, SCENE 2

The Forum.

[Enter BRUTUS and goes into the pulpit, and CASSIUS and the citizens]

CITIZENS   We demand an explanation!

BRUTUS   Follow me and listen, friends. Cassius, you go into the next street and separate mobs. Those who want an explanation, stay here. Those who want to go with Cassius, follow him. We will offer the public reasons for Caesar's assassination.

1ST CITIZEN   I want to hear Brutus.

2ND CITIZEN   I want to hear Cassius and compare the two speeches.

3RD CITIZEN   Quiet! The noble Brutus is ready to speak.

BRUTUS   Wait to the end before you respond. Romans, patriots, and friends, be quiet until I have explained my reason for joining the conspiracy. Trust my good reputation and believe that I tell the truth. Judge me wisely. Be alert that you may judge fairly. If any of you were Caesar's friend, I declare that your fondness for Caesar was no greater than mine. If you demand an explanation of my revolt against Caesar, this is my reply: Not that I didn't love Caesar, but that I loved Rome more. Would you prefer that Caesar still be a living tyrant or that he be dead and you Romans all free? Because he was a friend, I mourn him. Because he was lucky, I am happy for him. Because he was brave, I honor him. But, because he was ambitious, I assassinated him. His friendship deserved my love, his good fortune earned my regard. I honor his courage, but I slaughtered his ambition. Is there anyone here who would choose to be a slave? If there is, I have offended you. Is there anyone here who would choose not to be a Roman. If there is, I have offended you. Who is here so despicable that you have no patriotism? If there is, I have offended you. I await your answer.

ALL	None, Brutus, none!
BRUTUS	Then none have I offended. I have done no more to Caesar than you shall do to Brutus. The question of his death is enrolled in the Capitol; his glory not extenuated, wherein he was worthy; nor his offenses enforced, for which he suffered death. / *[Enter MARK ANTONY and others, with CAESAR'S body]* Here comes his body, mourned by Mark Antony, who, though he had no hand in his death, shall receive the benefit of his dying, a place in the commonwealth, as which of you shall not? With this I depart, that, as I slew my best lover for the good of Rome, I have the same dagger for myself when it shall please my country to need my death.
ALL	Live, Brutus! Live, live!
1ST CITIZEN	Bring him with triumph home unto his house.
2ND CITIZEN	Give him a statue with his ancestors.
3RD CITIZEN	Let him be Caesar.
4TH CITIZEN	Caesar's better parts Shall be crowned in Brutus.
1ST CITIZEN	We'll bring him to his house with shouts and clamours.
BRUTUS	My countrymen—
2ND CITIZEN	Peace! Silence! Brutus speaks,
1ST CITIZEN	Peace, ho!
BRUTUS	Good countrymen, let me depart alone, And for my sake, stay here with Antony. Do grace to Caesar's corse, and grace his speech Tending to Caesar's glories which Mark Antony, By our permission, is allowed to make. I do entreat you, not a man depart, Save I alone, till Antony have spoke. *[Exit]*
1ST CITIZEN	Stay, ho! and let us hear Mark Antony.
3RD CITIZEN	Let him go up into the public chair. We'll hear him, noble Antony, go up.
ANTONY	For Brutus sake I am beholding to you. *[ANTONY goes into the pulpit]*

Line numbers: 40, 45, 50, 55, 60, 65

ORIGINAL

ALL	No one, Brutus, no one!
BRUTUS	Therefore, no one takes offense. I have done no more harm to Caesar than you would do to me. The reason for his assassination is recorded at the Capitol. His victories are well stated explaining his value to Rome. None of the offenses leading to his assassination have been overstated. *[Enter MARK ANTONY and others, with CAESAR'S body]* Here comes Mark Antony with Caesar's corpse. Antony had no part in the assassination, but he will benefit from Caesar's death. He will have a place in the government, as all of you shall. I conclude now with this statement: As I killed my best friend for Rome's benefit, I offer you the same dagger to kill me when Rome shall demand my execution.
ALL	Live, Brutus! Live, live!
1ST CITIZEN	Send him home with a triumphal parade.
2ND CITIZEN	Place his statue among those of his ancestors.
3RD CITIZEN	Proclaim him the next Caesar.
4TH CITIZEN	Brutus shall be king for having Caesar's best qualities.
1ST CITIZEN	We will escort him home with celebration.
BRUTUS	Fellow Romans—
2ND CITIZEN	Quiet! Brutus is speaking.
1ST CITIZEN	Quiet!
BRUTUS	Fellow patriots, let me leave you to listen to Antony's speech. Be courteous to Caesar's remains and be gracious to Antony's funeral speech. We are allowing Antony to speak. I beg you, stay here while I leave. Remain to hear Antony. *[BRUTUS goes out]*
1ST CITIZEN	Stay and listen to Mark Antony.
3RD CITIZEN	Let Antony step up to the public lectern. We will listen, Antony.
ANTONY	For Brutus' sake, I owe you my thanks. *[ANTONY goes into the pulpit]*

TRANSLATION

4TH CITIZEN   What does he say of Brutus?

3RD CITIZEN   He says for Brutus' sake
He finds himself beholding to us all.   70

4TH CITIZEN   'Twere best he speak no harm of Brutus here!

1ST CITIZEN   This Caesar was a tyrant.

3RD CITIZEN   Nay, that's certain.
We are blest that Rome is rid of him.

2ND CITIZEN   Peace! Let us hear what Antony can say.

ANTONY   You gentle Romans—

ALL   Peace, ho! Let us hear him.   75

ANTONY   Friends, Romans, countrymen, lend me your ears;
I come to bury Caesar, not to praise him.
The evil that men do lives after them;
The good is oft interred with their bones.
So let it be with Caesar. The noble Brutus   80
Hath told you Caesar was ambitious.
If it were so, it was a grievous fault,
And grievously hath Caesar answered it.
Here under leave of Brutus and the rest
(For Brutus is an honourable man;   85
So are they all, all honourable men),
Come I to speak in Caesar's funeral.
He was my friend, faithful and just to me;
But Brutus says he was ambitious,
And Brutus is an honourable man.   90
He hath brought many captives home to Rome,
Whose ransoms did the general coffers fill.
Did this in Caesar seem ambitious?
When that the poor have cried, Caesar hath wept;
Ambition should be made of sterner stuff.   95
Yet Brutus says he was ambitious;
And Brutus is an honourable man.
You all did see that on the Lupercal
I thrice presented him a kingly crown,
Which he did thrice refuse. Was this ambition?   100
Yet Brutus says he was ambitious;
And sure he is an honourable man.
I speak not to disprove what Brutus spoke,
But here I am to speak what I do know.
You all did love him once, not without cause.   105

ORIGINAL

4TH CITIZEN	What did he say about Brutus?
3RD CITIZEN	He says that, for Brutus' sake, he owes us his thanks.
4TH CITIZEN	He had better not criticize Brutus!
1ST CITIZEN	Caesar was a tyrant.
3RD CITIZEN	He surely was. Rome is better off without him.
2ND CITIZEN	Quiet! Let us hear Antony's remarks.
ANTONY	You kind Romans—
ALL	Quiet! Let us hear him.
ANTONY	Friends, Roman, patriots, listen to me. I come to bury Caesar, not to praise him. Men's faults often outlive them while their good qualities are buried in the earth. So let Caesar's faults survive him. Brutus has said that Caesar was ambitious. It was a grievous fault, and Caesar has suffered a grievous punishment. With the permission of Brutus and the other conspirators (all of whom are honorable), I come to speak at Caesar's funeral. Caesar was my friend, loyal and fair to me. But Brutus says he was ambitious, and Brutus is honorable. Caesar has brought prisoners of war to Rome and ransomed them for cash to fill the nation's treasury. Did this act seem like ambition? When the poor wept, Caesar cried for them. Ambition should be tougher. But Brutus says that Caesar was ambitious, and Brutus is honorable. You observed on the feast of the Lupercal that I offered Caesar a crown, which he refused each time. Was this the act of an ambitious man? But Brutus says that Caesar was ambitious, and Brutus is honorable. I don't dispute Brutus' words. I can only speak what I know. You once loved Caesar for good reason.

ACT III

What cause withholds you then to mourn for him?
O judgment, thou art fled to brutish beasts,
And men have lost their reason! Bear with me.
My heart is in the coffin there with Caesar,
And I must pause till it come back to me.   110

1ST CITIZEN   Methinks there is much reason in his sayings.

2ND CITIZEN   If thou consider rightly of the matter,
Caesar has had great wrong.

3RD CITIZEN   Has he, masters?
I fear there will a worse come in his place.

4TH CITIZEN   Marked ye his words? He would not take the crown;   115
Therefore 'tis certain he was not ambitious.

1ST CITIZEN   If it be found so, some will dear abide it.

2ND CITIZEN   Poor soul! His eyes are red as fire with weeping.

3RD CITIZEN   There's not a nobler man in Rome than Antony.

4TH CITIZEN   Now mark him. He begins again to speak.   120

ANTONY   But yesterday the word of Caesar might
Have stood against the world. Now lies he there,
And none so poor to do him reverence.
O masters! If I were disposed to stir
Your hearts and minds to mutiny and rage,   125
I should do Brutus wrong, and Cassius wrong,
Who, you all know, are honourable men.
I will not do them wrong. I rather choose
To wrong the dead, to wrong myself and you,
Than I will wrong such honourable men. /   130
But here's a parchment with the seal of Caesar.
I found it in his closet; 'tis his will.
Let but the commons hear this testament,
Which (pardon me) I do not mean to read,
And they would go and kiss dead Caesar's wounds   135
And dip their napkins in his sacred blood;
Yea, beg a hair of him for memory,
And dying, mention it within their wills,
Bequeathing it as a rich legacy
Unto their issue.   140

4TH CITIZEN   We'll hear the will! Read it, Mark Antony.

ALL   The will, the will! We will hear Caesar's will!

ORIGINAL

Why don't you grieve for him? Men have lost their good judgment and act like brutes. Wait a bit. I am overcome with grief for Caesar and I must regain my composure.

1ST CITIZEN	Antony makes sense.
2ND CITIZEN	If you agree with him, then Caesar has been wronged.
3RD CITIZEN	I fear that a worse tyrant will replace him.
4TH CITIZEN	Did you hear Antony's words? Caesar didn't want to be king. He wasn't ambitious.
1ST CITIZEN	If we discover that he wasn't ambitious, the conspirators will pay for their mistake.
2ND CITIZEN	Poor man, his eyes are fiery red from crying.
3RD CITIZEN	Antony is the noblest man in Rome.
4TH CITIZEN	Look. He is speaking again.
ANTONY	Yesterday, Caesar might have given orders to the world. Now he lies here with no one to respect him. Oh masters! If I wanted to enrage you, I would wrong Brutus and Cassius, who, as you know, are honorable. I won't dishonor them. I would rather dishonor the dead or myself or you than to dishonor such honorable men. Here is a document sealed by Caesar. I found it in his office. It is his will. If ordinary citizens heard this will, which I don't intend to read, they would kiss Caesar's wounds and dip their handkerchiefs in his blood. They would ask for one of his hairs and bequeath it as a legacy to their children.

ACT III

4TH CITIZEN	Read the will, Mark Antony.
ALL	The will. We want to hear Caesar's will!

TRANSLATION

ANTONY	Have patience, gentle friends; I must not read it.
	It is not meet you know how Caesar loved you.
	You are not wood, you are not stones, but men; 145
	And being men, hearing the will of Caesar,
	It will inflame you, it will make you mad.
	'Tis good you know not that you are his heirs;
	For if you should, O, what would come of it?
4TH CITIZEN	Read the will! We'll hear it, Antony! 150
	You shall read us the will, Caesar's will!
ANTONY	Will you be patient? Will you stay awhile?
	I have o'ershot myself to tell you of it.
	I fear I wrong the honourable men
	Whose daggers have stabbed Caesar; I do fear it. 155
4TH CITIZEN	They were traitors. Honourable men!
ALL	The will! The testament!
2ND CITIZEN	They were villains, murderers! The will! Read the will!
ANTONY	You will compel me then to read the will?
	Then make a ring about the corse of Caesar 160
	And let me show you him that made the will.
	Shall I descend? and will you give me leave?
ALL	Come down.
2ND CITIZEN	Descend.
3RD CITIZEN	You shall have leave. 165
	[ANTONY comes down]
4TH CITIZEN	A ring! Stand round.
1ST CITIZEN	Stand from the hearse! Stand from the body!
2ND CITIZEN	Room for Antony, most noble Antony!
ANTONY	Nay, press not so upon me. Stand far off.
ALL	Stand back! Room! Bear back! 170

ANTONY	Be patient, friends. I must not read it. You should not know how much Caesar loved you. You are flesh rather than wood or stone. Being human and hearing the will, you will grow angry and outraged. It is good that you don't know that you are Caesar's heirs. If you knew that, what might happen?
4TH CITIZEN	Read the will to us, Antony! Read us Caesar's will!
ANTONY	Please be patient. Will you remain? I have revealed too much about the will. I fear I have wronged the honorable men who assassinated Caesar.
4TH CITIZEN	There were traitors, not honorable men!
ALL	The will! The document!
2ND CITIZEN	They were criminals, murderers! Read the will!
ANTONY	Are you forcing me to read the will? Form a circle around Caesar's body and look at the man who made you his heirs. Shall I come down? Will you allow me?
ALL	Come down.
2ND CITIZEN	Descend.
3RD CITIZEN	We will allow it. *[ANTONY comes down]*
4TH CITIZEN	Make a ring! Stand around the body.
1ST CITIZEN	Move back from the body! Move back!
2ND CITIZEN	Give Antony room!
ANTONY	Don't crowd around.
ALL	Move back! Give him room!

ACT III

ANTONY	If you have tears, prepare to shed them now.
	You all do know this mantle. I remember
	The first time ever Caesar put it on.
	'Twas on a summer's evening in his tent.
	That day he overcame the Nervii. 175
	Look, in this place ran Cassius' dagger through.
	See what a rent the envious Casca made.
	Through this the well beloved Brutus stabbed;
	And as he plucked his cursed steel away,
	Mark how the blood of Caesar followed it, 180
	As rushing out of doors to be resolved
	If Brutus so unkindly knocked or no;
	For Brutus, as you know, was Caesar's angel.
	Judge, O you gods, how dearly Caesar loved him!
	This was the most unkindest cut of all; 185
	For when the noble Caesar saw him stab,
	Ingratitude, more strong than traitors' arms,
	Quite vanquished him. Then burst his mighty heart;
	And in his mantle muffling up his face,
	Even at the base of Pompey's statue 190
	(Which all the while ran blood) great Caesar fell.
	O what a fall was there, my countrymen!
	Then I and you, and all of us fell down,
	Whilst bloody treason flourished over us.
	O, now you weep, and I perceive you feel 195
	The dint of pity. These are gracious drops.
	Kind souls, what weep you when you but behold
	Our Caesar's vesture wounded? Look you here!
	Here is himself, marred as you see with traitors.
1ST CITIZEN	O piteous spectacle! 200
2ND CITIZEN	O noble Caesar!
3RD CITIZEN	O woeful day!
4TH CITIZEN	O traitors, villains!
1ST CITIZEN	O most bloody sight!
2ND CITIZEN	We will be revenged. 205
ALL	Revenge! About! Sneak! Burn! Fire! Kill! Slay!
	Let not a traitor live!
ANTONY	Stay, countrymen.
1ST CITIZEN	Peace there! Hear the noble Antony.
2ND CITIZEN	We'll hear him, we'll follow him, we'll die with him! 210

ORIGINAL

ANTONY	If you feel sorrow, prepare to weep. You recognize this cloak. I remember the first time that Caesar wore it. It was on a summer evening in his tent the day he defeated the Nervii in Gaul. Look at this hole that Cassius made with his dagger. See how Casca tore the cloak. This is where his good friend Brutus stabbed. When he pulled out his blade, see how the blood flowed, as though trying to ask Brutus why he attacked his friend. You know, Caesar thought that Brutus was an angel. Judge, Oh gods, how much Caesar loved him. This was the most undeserved stab. When Caesar saw Brutus attacking him, Caesar was overcome by Brutus' disloyalty. Then Caesar's great heart burst and, wrapped in his cloak, he collapsed at the foot of Pompey's statue (which was covered in blood). Oh what a loss it was, my fellow Romans! Then we all suffered a blow of savage treason. I see that you are weeping out of pity. These are generous tears. Kind souls, how you weep over Caesar's damaged cloak. Look at his body! Here is Caesar himself punctured by traitors.

ACT III

1ST CITIZEN	Oh sad sight!
2ND CITIZEN	Oh noble Caesar!
3RD CITIZEN	Oh wretched day!
4TH CITIZEN	Oh traitors, criminals!
1ST CITIZEN	Oh bloody corpse!
2ND CITIZEN	We want revenge.
ALL	Vengeance! Let's burn and murder the traitors. Let none of them survive.
ANTONY	Wait, Romans.
1ST CITIZEN	Quiet there! Listen to Antony.
2ND CITIZEN	We will listen and follow him. We will die with him!

TRANSLATION

ANTONY	Good friends, sweet friends, let me not stir you up
	To such a sudden flood of mutiny.
	They that have done this deed are honourable.
	What private griefs they have, alas, I know not,
	That made them do it. They are wise and honourable, 215
	And will no doubt with reasons answer you.
	I came not, friends, to steal away your hearts.
	I am no orator, as Brutus is,
	But (as you know me all) a plain blunt man
	That love my friend; and that they know full well 220
	That gave me public leave to speak of him.
	For I have neither writ, nor words, nor worth,
	Action, nor utterance, nor the power of speech
	To stir men's blood. I only speak right on.
	I tell you that which you yourselves do know, 225
	Show you sweet Caesar's wounds, poor poor dumb mouths,
	And bid them speak for me. But were I Brutus,
	And Brutus Antony, there were an Antony
	Would ruffle up your spirits, and put a tongue
	In every wound of Caesar that should move 230
	The stones of Rome to rise and mutiny.
ALL	We'll mutiny.
1ST CITIZEN	We'll burn the house of Brutus.
3RD CITIZEN	Away then! Come, seek the conspirators.
ANTONY	Yet hear me, countrymen. Yet hear me speak.
ALL	Peace, ho! Hear Antony, most noble Antony! 235
ANTONY	Why friends, you go to do you know not what.
	Wherein hath Caesar thus deserved your loves?
	Alas, you know not! I must tell you then.
	You have forgot the will I told you of.
ALL	Most true! The will! Let's stay and hear the will. 240
ANTONY	Here is the will, and under Caesar's seal.
	To every Roman citizen he gives,
	To every several man, seventy-five drachmas.
2ND CITIZEN	Most noble Caesar! We'll revenge his death.
3RD CITIZEN	O royal Caesar! 245
ANTONY	Hear me with patience.
ALL	Peace, ho!

ANTONY	Friends, don't let me arouse you to revolt. The conspirators are honorable. I don't know what private reasons made them assassinate Caesar. They are wise and respected and will probably give you reasons for this deed. I didn't come to make you cry. I'm not so polished a speaker as Brutus. As you know, I am a plain man. I loved my friend. The conspirators allowed me to speak of Caesar. I have no speech nor words nor skill at oratory. I speak plain truth. I remind you of what you already know, and I reveal Caesar's gaping wounds. If I were as skillful as Brutus, I would fire your spirits to revolt.

ACT III

ALL	We will rebel.
1ST CITIZEN	We'll burn Brutus' house.
2RD CITIZEN	Come, let's hunt the conspirators.
ANTONY	Let me finish, patriots. Let me speak.
ALL	Quiet! Listen to Antony!
ANTONY	You are about to do the unthinkable. Why did Caesar deserve your love? You don't yet know. I haven't read the will.
ALL	Yes! Let's listen to a reading of the will.
ANTONY	Here is the document sealed by Caesar. To each Roman he leaves $30, about 2 weeks' pay.
2ND CITIZEN	Most noble Caesar! We will avenge his loss.
3RD CITIZEN	Oh kingly Caesar!
ANTONY	Be patient.
ALL	Quiet!

TRANSLATION

ANTONY	Moreover he hath left you all his walks,
	His private arbors, and new-planted orchards,
	On this side Tiber; he hath left them you, 250
	And to your heirs for ever—common pleasures,
	To walk abroad and recreate yourselves.
	Here was a Caesar! When comes such another?
1ST CITIZEN	Never, never! Come away, away!
	We'll burn his body in the holy place 255
	And with the brands fire the traitors' houses.
	Take up the body.
2ND CITIZEN	Go fetch fire!
3RD CITIZEN	Pluck down benches!
4TH CITIZEN	Pluck down forms, windows, anything! 260
	[Exit citizens with the body]
ANTONY	Now let it work. Mischief, thou art afoot,
	Take thou what course thou wilt.
	[Enter a Servant]
	How now, fellow?
SERVANT	Sir, Octavius is already come to Rome.
ANTONY	Where is he?
SERVANT	He and Lepidus are at Caesar's house. 265
ANTONY	And thither will I straight to visit him.
	He comes upon a wish. Fortune is merry,
	And in this mood will give us anything.
SERVANT	I heard him say Brutus and Cassius
	Are rid like madmen through the gates of Rome. 270
ANTONY	Belike they had some notice of the people,
	How I had moved them. Bring me to Octavius. *[Exeunt]*

ANTONY	For public recreation, he left his walkways, arbors, and orchards on this side of the Tiber River. Here was a great man! When will we see another?
1ST CITIZEN	Never! Come, let's burn his body and set fire to the conspirators' homes. Bring the body.
2ND CITIZEN	Bring fire!
3RD CITIZEN	Pile up benches!
4TH CITIZEN	Pull down frameworks, shutters, anything that will burn! *[Exit citizens with the body]*
ANTONY	Now let it work. Mischief, you are underway. Go wherever you want. *[Enter a Servant]* What is it?
SERVANT	Sir, Octavius has arrived.
ANTONY	Where is he?
SERVANT	He and Lepidus are at Caesar's house.
ANTONY	I will go straight to Octavius. He comes just as I wanted. Luck and the public mood will give us whatever we wish.
SERVANT	I heard Octavius say that Brutus and Cassius have galloped madly out of Rome.
ANTONY	Probably because they observed the mob that I aroused. Take me to Octavius. *[They go out]*

ACT III

TRANSLATION

ACT III, SCENE 3

Rome, a street.

[Enter CINNA the Poet, and after him the citizens]

CINNA	I dreamt to-night that I did feast with Caesar,	
	And things unluckily charge my fantasy.	
	I have no will to wander forth of doors,	
	Yet something leads me forth.	
1ST CITIZEN	What is your name?	5
2ND CITIZEN	Whither are you going?	
3RD CITIZEN	Where do you dwell?	
4TH CITIZEN	Are you a married man or a bachelor?	
2ND CITIZEN	Answer every man directly.	
1ST CITIZEN	Ay, and briefly.	10
4TH CITIZEN	Ay, and wisely.	
3RD CITIZEN	Ay, and truly, you were best.	
CINNA	What is my name? Whither am I going?	
	Where do I dwell? Am I a married man or a	
	bachelor? Then, to answer every man directly and	15
	briefly, wisely and truly: wisely I say, I am a	
	bachelor.	
2ND CITIZEN	That's as much as to say they are	
	fools that marry. You'll bear me a bang for that,	
	I fear. Proceed directly.	20
CINNA	Directly I am going to Caesar's funeral.	
1ST CITIZEN	As a friend or an enemy?	
CINNA	As a friend.	
2ND CITIZEN	That matter is answered directly.	
4TH CITIZEN	For your dwelling—briefly.	25
CINNA	Briefly, I dwell by the Capitol.	
3RD CITIZEN	Your name, sir, truly.	
CINNA	Truly, my name is Cinna.	

ORIGINAL

ACT III, SCENE 3

Rome, a street.

[Enter CINNA the Poet, and after him the citizens]

CINNA	I dreamed last night that I ate dinner with Caesar and fell upon bad luck. I don't want to be outdoors, but something pushes me forward.
1ST CITIZEN	Who are you?
2ND CITIZEN	Where are you going?
3RD CITIZEN	Where do you live?
4TH CITIZEN	Are you married or single?
2ND CITIZEN	Answer us.
1ST CITIZEN	Yes, and be brief.
4TH CITIZEN	And be sensible.
3RD CITIZEN	And tell the truth.
CINNA	Who am I? Where am I going? Where do I live? Am I married or single? To answer directly, briefly, sensibly, and truthfully, I am single.
2ND CITIZEN	You imply that only fools marry. I'll pound you for that. Go on.
CINNA	I am going to Caesar's funeral.
1ST CITIZEN	Were you his friend or his enemy?
CINNA	His friend.
2ND CITIZEN	That's a simple answer.
4TH CITIZEN	Your home?
CINNA	I live near the Capitol.
3RD CITIZEN	Your name?
CINNA	I am Cinna.

ACT III

TRANSLATION

1ST CITIZEN	Tear him to pieces! He's a conspirator.
CINNA	I am Cinna the poet! I am Cinna the poet!
4TH CITIZEN	Tear him for his bad verses! Tear him for his bad verses!
CINNA	I am not Cinna the conspirator.
4TH CITIZEN	It is no matter; his name's Cinna! Pluck but his name out of his heart, and turn him going.
3RD CITIZEN	Tear him, tear him! *[They kill him]* Come, brands ho! firebrands! To Brutus', to Cassius'! Burn all! Some to Decius' house and some to Casca's; some to Ligarius'! Away, go! *[Exeunt citizens with the body of CINNA]*

1ST CITIZEN	Destroy him. He's a conspirator.
CINNA	I am Cinna the poet! I am Cinna the poet!
4TH CITIZEN	Strike him for his bad poetry! Strike him for his bad poetry!
CINNA	I am not Cinna the conspirator.
4TH CITIZEN	It doesn't matter. Rip out his heart and send him on his way.
3RD CITIZEN	Strike him! Strike him! *[They murder CINNA the poet]* Come with torches! To Brutus and Cassius' houses! Burn everything. Some go to Decius, Casca, and Ligarius' homes. Let's go! *[The mob departs with the body of CINNA the poet]*

ACT III

ACT IV, SCENE 1

Rome, a room in Antony's house.

[Enter ANTONY, OCTAVIUS, and LEPIDUS]

ANTONY   These many, then, shall die; their names are pricked.

OCTAVIUS   Your brother too must die. Consent you, Lepidus?

LEPIDUS   I do consent—

OCTAVIUS   Prick him down, Antony.

LEPIDUS   Upon condition Publius shall not live,
Who is your sister's son, Mark Antony.   5

ANTONY   He shall not live. Look, with a spot I damn him.
But, Lepidus, go you to Caesar's house.
Fetch the will hither, and we shall determine
How to cut off some charge in legacies.

LEPIDUS   What, shall I find you here?   10

OCTAVIUS   Or here or at the Capitol. *[Exit LEPIDUS]*

ANTONY   This is a slight unmeritable man,
Meet to be sent on errands. Is it fit,
The threefold world divided, he should stand
One of the three to share it?

OCTAVIUS   So you thought him,   15
And took his voice who should be pricked to die
In our black sentence and proscription.

ANTONY   Octavius, I have seen more days than you;
And though we lay these honours on this man
To ease ourselves of divers sland'rous loads,   20
He shall but bear them as the ass bears gold,
To groan and sweat under the business,
Either led or driven as we point the way;
And having brought our treasure where we will,
Then take we down his load, and turn him off   25
(Like to the empty ass) to shake his ears
And graze in commons.

OCTAVIUS   You may do your will;
But he's a tried and valiant soldier.

ACT IV, SCENE 1

Rome, a room in Antony's house.

[Enter ANTONY, OCTAVIUS, and LEPIDUS]

ANTONY   We must execute these people. I have checked off their names.

OCTAVIUS   Your brother also must die. Do you agree, Lepidus?

LEPIDUS   I agree.

OCTAVIUS   Check his name off the list, Antony.

LEPIDUS   I insist that we must kill Publius, who is your sister's son, Mark Antony.

ANTONY   He must die. See, I checked his name. Lepidus, go to Caesar's house and bring the will. We will decide how to block the heirs from receiving legacies.

LEPIDUS   Shall I return here for you?

OCTAVIUS   Either here or at the Capitol. *[LEPIDUS goes out]*

ANTONY   This is a worthless man suited to going on errands. Is it right that he should control one-third of the Roman world?

OCTAVIUS   You chose him and you took his advice about which Romans should be executed.

ANTONY   Octavius, I am older than you. Although we chose Lepidus to rid ourselves of scandal, he will work for us like a mule bearing gold in whatever direction we point. When he has delivered treasure to us, then we will rid ourselves of him and put him out to pasture.

OCTAVIUS   Do whatever you wish, but remember that he is an experienced, courageous soldier.

ACT IV

TRANSLATION

ANTONY	So is my horse, Octavius, and for that
	I do appoint him store of provender. 30
	It is a creature that I teach to fight,
	To wind, to stop, to run directly on,
	His corporal motion governed by my spirit.
	And, in some taste, is Lepidus but so.
	He must be taught, and trained, and bid go forth: 35
	A barren-spirited fellow; one that feeds
	On objects, arts, and imitations
	Which, out of use and staled by other men,
	Begin his fashion. Do not talk of him
	But as a property. And now, Octavius, 40
	Listen great things. Brutus and Cassius
	Are levying powers. We must straight make head.
	Therefore let our alliance be combined,
	Our best friends made, or means stretched;
	And let us presently go sit in council 45
	How covert matters may be best disclosed
	And open perils surest answered.
OCTAVIUS	Let us do so; for we are at the stake
	And bayed about with many enemies;
	And some that smile have in their hearts, I fear, 50
	Millions of mischiefs. *[Exeunt]*

ANTONY   So is my horse, Octavius, and for that I feed him well. I teach him to fight, turn, halt, and charge as I command. Lepidus is like my horse. We must teach and train him and send him on errands. He is dull and lacking in taste. He follows fads. Think of him only as a possession. Octavius, I have great news. Brutus and Cassius are hiring soldiers. We must do the same. Let's strengthen our alliance and make new allies to fill our needs. Let's meet to discuss secret matters and obvious dangers.

OCTAVIUS   Good idea. We are surrounded by enemies like a bear threatened by hounds. I am afraid that some who appear to agree with us conceal their own plots. *[They go out]*

ACT IV

ACT IV, SCENE 2

Before Brutus' tent near Sardis.

[Drum. Enter BRUTUS, LUCILIUS, LUCIUS, and the army. TITINIUS and PINDARUS meet them]

BRUTUS   Stand ho!

LUCILIUS   Give the word, ho! and stand!

BRUTUS   What now, Lucilius? Is Cassius near?

LUCILIUS   He is at hand, and Pindarus is come
To do you salutation from his master.   5

BRUTUS   He greets me well. Your master, Pindarus,
In his own change, or by ill officers,
Hath given me some worthy cause to wish
Things done undone; but if he be at hand,
I shall be satisfied.

PINDARUS   I do not doubt   10
But that my noble master will appear
Such as he is, full of regard and honour.

BRUTUS   He is not doubted. A word, Lucilius,
How he received you. Let me be resolved.

LUCILIUS   With courtesy and with respect enough,   15
But not with such familiar instances
Nor with such free and friendly conference
As he hath used of old.

BRUTUS   Thou hast described
A hot friend cooling. Ever note, Lucilius,
When love begins to sicken and decay   20
It useth an enforced ceremony.
There are no tricks in plain and simple faith;
But hollow men, like horses hot at hand,
Make gallant show and promise of their mettle;
[Low march within]
But when they should endure the bloody spur,   25
They fall their crests, and like deceitful jades
Sink in the trial. Comes his army on?

ORIGINAL

ACT IV, SCENE 2

In front of Brutus' tent near Sardis in Turkey.

[At the sound of a drum, BRUTUS, LUCILIUS, LUCIUS, and the army enter and meet TITINIUS and PINDARUS]

BRUTUS   Stand at attention.

LUCILIUS   Pass the word to stand at attention.

BRUTUS   What news do you bring, Lucilius? Is Cassius coming?

LUCILIUS   He is approaching. And Pindarus has brought greetings from his master, Cassius.

BRUTUS   He is courteous. Pindarus, your master has given me cause to complain. If he is approaching, I will discuss it with him.

PINDARUS   I am sure that Cassius will arrive soon. He is dependable and honorable.

BRUTUS   I don't doubt him. Lucilius, tell me how Cassius received you. I need to know.

LUCILIUS   He was polite and courteous, but he lacked the freedom and friendliness that he used to have.

BRUTUS   You are describing the cooling of a friendship. Have you ever noticed, Lucilius, that when friendships weaken, our old friends behave with forced politeness. Honest faith requires no trickery. But insincere men, like spirited horses, put on a display of gallantry and courage. *[A muffled drum indicates soldiers marching from a distance]* When horses should tolerate spurs, they droop their heads and fall back. Is Cassius' army nearby?

ACT IV

LUCILIUS	They mean this night in Sardis to be quartered.
	The greater part, the horse in general,
	Are come with Cassius.
BRUTUS	Hark! He is arrived. 30
	March gently on to meet him.
	[Enter CASSIUS and his powers]
CASSIUS	Stand ho!
BRUTUS	Stand ho! and speak the word along.
1ST SOLDIER	Stand!
2ND SOLDIER	Stand! 35
3RD SOLDIER	Stand!
CASSIUS	Most noble brother, you have done me wrong.
BRUTUS	Judge me, you gods! wrong I mine enemies?
	And if not so, how should I wrong a brother?
CASSIUS	Brutus, this sober form of yours hides wrongs; 40
	And when you do them—
BRUTUS	Cassius, be content.
	Speak your griefs softly. I do know you well.
	Before the eyes of both our armies here
	(Which should perceive nothing but love from us)
	Let us not wrangle. Bid them move away. 45
	Then in my tent, Cassius, enlarge your griefs,
	And I will give you audience.
CASSIUS	Pindarus,
	Bid our commanders lead their charges off
	A little from this ground.
BRUTUS	Lucilius, do you the like; and let no man 50
	Come to our tent till we have done our conference.
	Let Lucius and Titinius guard our door. *[Exeunt]*

ORIGINAL

LUCILIUS	They plan to camp at Sardis tonight. The cavalry has already arrived with Cassius.
BRUTUS	Look, he is here. Go out courteously to meet him. *[CASSIUS enters along with his staff of officers]*
CASSIUS	Stand at attention.
BRUTUS	Stand at attention and pass the word to the other soldiers.
1ST SOLDIER	Attention!
2ND SOLDIER	Attention!
3RD SOLDIER	Attention!
CASSIUS	Noble comrade, you have wronged me.
BRUTUS	Before God, have I even wronged my enemies? If I haven't, why would I wrong a comrade?
CASSIUS	Brutus, you conceal wrongdoing under a stern face. When you are at fault—
BRUTUS	Cassius, cool down. Tell me your complaints. I know you well. We shouldn't quarrel in front of our armies. They should see nothing but agreement between us. Send them away. Then come to my tent, Cassius, state your complaints and I will listen.
CASSIUS	Pindarus, have our officers move the army away from here.
BRUTUS	Lucilius, do the same with my army. Don't allow soldiers to come to our tent until we have finished discussing matters. Send Lucius and Titinius to guard the entrance. *[They depart]*

ACT IV

TRANSLATION

ACT IV, SCENE 3

Within Brutus' tent.

[Enter BRUTUS and CASSIUS]

CASSIUS
That you have wronged me doth appear in this:
You have condemned and noted Lucius Pella
For taking bribes here of the Sardians;
Wherein my letters, praying on his side,
Because I knew the man, was slighted off.   5

BRUTUS
You wronged yourself to write in such a case.

CASSIUS
In such a time as this it is not meet
That every nice offence should bear his comment.

BRUTUS
Let me tell you, Cassius, you yourself
Are much condemned to have an itching palm,   10
To sell and mart your offices for gold
To undeservers.

CASSIUS
                I an itching palm?
You know that you are Brutus that speaks this,
Or by the gods, this speech were else your last!

BRUTUS
The name of Cassius honours this corruption   15
And chastisement doth therefore hide his head.

CASSIUS
Chastisement?

BRUTUS
Remember March; the ides of March remember.
Did not great Julius bleed for justice sake?
What villain touched his body that did stab   20
And not for justice? What, shall one of us,
That struck the foremost man of all this world
But for supporting robbers—shall we now
Contaminate our fingers with base bribes,
And sell the mighty space of our large honours   25
For so much trash as may be grasped thus?
I had rather be a dog and bay the moon
Than such a Roman.

CASSIUS
              Brutus, bait not me!
I'll not endure it. You forget yourself
To hedge me in. I am a soldier, I,   30
Older in practice, abler than yourself
To make conditions.

ORIGINAL

ACT IV, SCENE 3

Within Brutus' tent.

[Enter BRUTUS and CASSIUS]

CASSIUS   Here is my complaint against you: You condemned and disgraced Lucius Pella for taking bribes from the people of Sardis. When I wrote letters absolving him of wrong, you ignored me.

BRUTUS   You were wrong to interfere in the matter.

CASSIUS   In these difficult times, it is detrimental to criticize every small offense.

BRUTUS   I must add, Cassius, that you yourself have been charged with greed for selling appointments to undeserving men.

CASSIUS   Me, greedy? If anybody but Brutus charged me, by God, he would die!

BRUTUS   Because of your importance, the corruption goes uncorrected.

CASSIUS   Uncorrected?

BRUTUS   Remember March 15 and the reasons that we assassinated Caesar. Didn't Julius Caesar die for the sake of justice? What criminal helped us assassinate him for some other reason than justice? Shall one of the conspirators who stabbed the world's most important man for stealing Roman liberty now dirty his hands with common bribery? Shall we sell appointments for cash to put in our pockets? I would rather be a barking dog than so dishonorable a Roman.

CASSIUS   Brutus, don't try my patience! I won't tolerate it. You risk retaliation to accuse me. I am a more experienced and more skilled soldier than you for deciding matters.

BRUTUS Go to! You are not, Cassius.

CASSIUS I am.

BRUTUS I say you are not.

CASSIUS Urge me no more! I shall forget myself. 35
Have mind upon your health. Tempt me no further.

BRUTUS Away, slight man!

CASSIUS Is't possible?

BRUTUS Hear me, for I will speak.
Must I give way and room to your rash choler?
Shall I be frighted when a madman stares? 40

CASSIUS O ye gods, ye gods! Must I endure all this?

BRUTUS All this! Aye, more. Fret till your proud heart break.
Go show your slaves how choleric you are
And make your bondmen tremble. Must I budge?
Must I observe you? Must I stand and crouch 45
Under your testy humour? By the gods,
You shall digest the venom of your spleen,
Though it do split you; for from this day forth
I'll use you for my mirth, yea, for my laughter,
When you are waspish.

CASSIUS Is it come to this? 50

BRUTUS You say you are a better soldier.
Let it appear so; make your vaunting true,
And it shall please me well. For mine own part,
I shall be glad to learn of noble men.

CASSIUS You wrong me every way! You wrong me, Brutus! 55
I said an elder soldier, not a better.
Did I say 'better'?

BRUTUS If you did, I care not.

CASSIUS When Caesar lived he durst not thus have moved me.

BRUTUS Peace, peace! You durst not so have tempted him.

CASSIUS I durst not? 60

BRUTUS No.

CASSIUS What, durst not tempt him?

BRUTUS For your life, you durst not.

ORIGINAL

BRUTUS	Nonsense! You are not, Cassius.
CASSIUS	Yes I am.
BRUTUS	I say you aren't.
CASSIUS	Don't push me! I will lose control and threaten you. Don't tempt me.
BRUTUS	Go away, little man!
CASSIUS	Is it possible that you speak this way to me?
BRUTUS	Listen. Do I have to refrain from chiding you because of your hot temper? Should I be scared when a lunatic glares at me?
CASSIUS	Dear God! Do I have to listen to this?
BRUTUS	All this and more. Whimper until your pride is broken. Rage at your slaves and terrify your staff. Must I give in? Should I watch and say nothing? Should I stand at attention or cower under your crankiness? By God, you will swallow your anger, even if you split a gut. From now on, I will laugh at you when you are in a snit.
CASSIUS	Has our alliance come to this?
BRUTUS	You claim to be a better soldier. Then act like one. Make your boast come true and I will be content. As for me, I am happy to learn from a respectable man.
CASSIUS	You misjudge me in every way! You misjudge me, Brutus! I said I am an older soldier, not a better soldier. Did I say "better"?
BRUTUS	It doesn't matter.
CASSIUS	When Caesar was alive, he didn't dare challenge me like this.
BRUTUS	Hush. You wouldn't have challenged him.
CASSIUS	Wouldn't I?
BRUTUS	No.
CASSIUS	You don't think I would have challenged him?
BRUTUS	Not if you valued your life.

ACT IV

TRANSLATION

CASSIUS   Do not presume too much upon my love.
           I may do that I shall be sorry for.

BRUTUS   You have done that you should be sorry for.   65
           There is no terror, Cassius, in your threats;
           For I am armed so strong in honesty
           That they pass by me as the idle wind,
           Which I respect not. I did send to you
           For certain sums of gold, which you denied me;   70
           For I can raise no money by vile means.
           By heaven, I had rather coin my heart
           And drop my blood for drachmas than to wring
           From the hard hands of peasants their vile trash
           By any indirection. I did send   75
           To you for gold to pay my legions,
           Which you denied me. Was that done like Cassius?
           Should I have answered Caius Cassius so?
           When Marcus Brutus grows so covetous
           To lock such rascal counters from his friends,   80
           Be ready, gods, with all your thunderbolts,
           Dash him to pieces!

CASSIUS   I denied you not.

BRUTUS   You did.

CASSIUS   I did not. He was but a fool that brought
           My answer back. Brutus hath rived my heart.   85
           A friend should bear his friend's infirmities,
           But Brutus makes mine greater than they are.

BRUTUS   I do not, till you practise them on me.

CASSIUS   You love me not.

BRUTUS   I do not like your faults.

CASSIUS   A friendly eye could never see such faults.   90

BRUTUS   A flatterer's would not, though they do appear
           As high as huge Olympus.

CASSIUS	Don't think I'm so good a friend that I won't challenge you. I may do something that I will later regret.
BRUTUS	You have already done what you should regret. I'm not afraid of your threats, Cassius. I am so honest that your taunts blow by me like wind. I requested money, which you refused to give me. I won't raise money by selling appointments. I would rather turn my heart into coins than to extort money from peasants. I requested money to pay my army. You refused. Was your refusal honorable? Would I have refused you money for the same purpose? When I become so greedy that I deny cash to friends, be ready, Gods, to strike me with lightning!
CASSIUS	I didn't refuse your request.
BRUTUS	You did.
CASSIUS	I did not. The messenger that said I did was a fool. You have wounded my heart. A friend should tolerate a friend's weaknesses, but you exaggerate mine.
BRUTUS	I don't exaggerate your faults until they affect me personally.
CASSIUS	You detest me.
BRUTUS	I dislike your faults.
CASSIUS	A friend would ignore my faults.
BRUTUS	A flatterer would ignore them if they were piled up as high as Mount Olympus.

ACT IV

TRANSLATION

CASSIUS	Come, Antony, and young Octavius, come!
	Revenge yourselves alone on Cassius.
	For Cassius is aweary of the world: 95
	Hated by one he loves; braved by his brother;
	Checked like a bondman; all his faults observed,
	Set in a notebook, learned and conned by rote
	To cast into my teeth. O, I could weep
	My spirit from mine eyes! There is my dagger, 100
	And here my naked breast; within, a heart
	Dearer than Pluto's mine, richer than gold.
	If that thou be'st a Roman, take it forth.
	I, that denied thee gold, will give my heart.
	Strike as thou didst at Caesar; for I know, 105
	When thou didst hate him worst, thou lovedst him better
	Than ever thou lovedst Cassius.
BRUTUS	Sheathe your dagger.
	Be angry when you will; it shall have scope.
	Do what you will; dishonour shall be humour
	O Cassius, you are yoked with a lamb 110
	That carries anger as the flint bears fire;
	Who, much enforced, shows a hasty spark,
	And straight is cold again.
CASSIUS	Hath Cassius lived
	To be but mirth and laughter to his Brutus
	When grief and blood ill-tempered vexeth him? 115
BRUTUS	When I spoke that, I was ill-tempered too.
CASSIUS	Do you confess so much? Give me your hand.
BRUTUS	And my heart too.
CASSIUS	O Brutus!
BRUTUS	What's the matter?
CASSIUS	Have you not love enough to bear with me
	When that rash humour which my mother gave me 120
	Makes me forgetful?
BRUTUS	Yes, Cassius; and from henceforth,
	When you are over-earnest with your Brutus,
	He'll think your mother chides, and leave you so.
	[Enter a poet, followed by LUCILIUS, TITINIUS,
	and LUCIUS]

CASSIUS	Antony and Octavius should come here and attack me now. I am sick at heart. My comrade hates and defies me. I am lectured like a slave. All my faults listed in a note-book, memorized, and tossed back in my face. I could cry my eyes out! Here is my dagger and here my chest. Within is a heart more worthy than gold. If you are a patriot, take my heart from my chest if I refused your request for money. Stab me as you did Caesar. I know that, even though you detested him, you loved him more than you love me.
BRUTUS	Put up your dagger. You are free to be angry whenever you will. Do whatever you want. I will diagnose your behavior as moodiness. Cassius, you are partnered with a lamb who strikes anger into flame. Once a spark appears, I calm down.
CASSIUS	Do I live to make you laugh at my sorrow and immoder-ate temper?
BRUTUS	I admit that I was also out of control.
CASSIUS	Do you admit it? Let's shake hands.
BRUTUS	I pledge you my heart also.
CASSIUS	Oh Brutus!
BRUTUS	What?
CASSIUS	Aren't you willing to tolerate the reckless rage that I inherited from my mother?
BRUTUS	Yes, Cassius. From now on, when you are out of sorts with me, I will think of your mother and not scold you. *[Enter a poet, followed by LUCILIUS, TITINIUS, and LUCIUS]*

ACT IV

TRANSLATION

POET	Let me go in to see the generals!
	There is some grudge between 'em. 'Tis not meet 125
	They be alone.
LUCILIUS	You shall not come to them.
POET	Nothing but death shall stay me.
CASSIUS	How now? What's the matter?
POET	For shame, you generals! What do you mean? 130
	Love and be friends, as two such men should be;
	For I have seen more years, I'm sure, than ye.
CASSIUS	Ha ha! How vilely doth this cynic rhyme!
BRUTUS	Get you hence, sirrah! Saucy fellow, hence!
CASSIUS	Bear with him, Brutus. 'Tis his fashion. 135
BRUTUS	I'll know his humour when he knows his time.
	What should the wars do with these jigging fools?
	Companion, hence!
CASSIUS	Away, away, be gone!
	[Exit poet]
BRUTUS	Lucilius and Titinius, bid the commanders
	Prepare to lodge their companies to-night. 140
CASSIUS	And come yourselves, and bring Messala with you
	Immediately to us. *[Exeunt LUCIUS and TITINIUS]*
BRUTUS	Lucius, a bowl of wine.
	[Exit LUCIUS]
CASSIUS	I did not think you could have been so angry.
BRUTUS	O Cassius, I am sick of many griefs.
CASSIUS	Of your philosophy you make no use 145
	If you give place to accidental evils.
BRUTUS	No man bears sorrow better. Portia is dead.
CASSIUS	Ha! Portia?
BRUTUS	She is dead.
CASSIUS	How scaped I killing when I crossed you so? 150
	O insupportable and touching loss!
	Upon what sickness?

ORIGINAL

POET	Let me see Brutus and Cassius! They are quarreling. They should not be alone.
LUCILIUS	You can't go in.
POET	Nothing but the threat of death will stop me.
CASSIUS	What's this? What's the matter?
POET	You generals should be ashamed. Why are you quarreling? Be loving comrades, as two adults should be. I know because I am an old man.
CASSIUS	Ha ha! This poet makes petty rhymes.
BRUTUS	Out with you! Out, you rude fellow.
CASSIUS	Ignore him, Brutus. It is his habit.
BRUTUS	I'll analyze his mood later. Why would a poet follow soldiers to war? Out, rascal!
CASSIUS	Go away! *[The poet goes out]*
BRUTUS	Lucilius and Titinius, have the officers prepare the army to spend the night.
CASSIUS	Both of you come in and bring Messala with you. *[LUCIUS and TITINIUS depart]*
BRUTUS	Lucius, bring a pitcher of wine. *[LUCIUS goes out]*
CASSIUS	I didn't think you could be so angry.
BRUTUS	Oh Cassius, I am beset by sorrows.
CASSIUS	You violate your principles when you let these incidents rile you.
BRUTUS	No man bears sorrow better than I. Portia is dead.
CASSIUS	What? Portia?
BRUTUS	She died.
CASSIUS	How did you keep from killing me when I rebuked you? Oh terrible loss! From what illness?

ACT IV

TRANSLATION

BRUTUS   Impatient of my absence,
And grief that young Octavius with Mark Antony
Have made themselves so strong; for with her death
That tidings came. With this she fell distract,   155
And (her attendants absent) swallowed fire.

CASSIUS   And died so?

BRUTUS   Even so.

CASSIUS   O ye immortal gods!
[Enter LUCIUS with wine and tapers]

BRUTUS   Speak no more of her. Give me a bowl of wine. *[Drinks]*
In this I bury all unkindness, Cassius.

CASSIUS   My heart is thirsty for that noble pledge.   160
Fill, Lucius, till the wine o'erswell the cup.
I cannot drink too much of Brutus' love.
[Drinks. Exit LUCIUS]
[Enter TITINIUS and MESSALA]

BRUTUS   Come in, Titinius! Welcome, good Messala.
Now sit we close about this taper here
And call in question our necessities.   165

CASSIUS   Portia, art thou gone?

BRUTUS   No more, I pray you.
Messala, I have here received letters
That young Octavius and Mark Antony
Come down upon us with a mighty power,
Bending their expedition toward Philippi.   170

MESSALA   Myself have letters of the selfsame tenure.

BRUTUS   With what addition?

MESSALA   That by proscription and bills of outlawry
Octavius, Antony, and Lepidus
Have put to death an hundred senators.   175

BRUTUS   Therein our letters do not well agree.
Mine speak of seventy senators that died
By their proscriptions, Cicero being one.

CASSIUS   Cicero one?

MESSALA   Cicero is dead,
And by that order of proscription.   180
Had you your letters from your wife, my lord?

ORIGINAL

BRUTUS	She grieved for me. She also grieved for the growing power of Octavius and Mark Antony. I learned of their strength the same time that I heard of her death. She was depressed. While her maids were out, she swallowed hot coals.
CASSIUS	Did she die of it?
BRUTUS	Yes.
CASSIUS	Oh, Gods! *[Enter LUCIUS with wine and tapers]*
BRUTUS	Say no more about. Pour me a cup of wine, Lucius. *[Drinks]* With this drink, I abandon our quarrel, Cassius.
CASSIUS	I am eager to share the toast. Lucius, fill my cup to the brim. I can't drink enough of Brutus' friendship. *[Drinks. LUCIUS goes out] [TITINIUS and MESSALA enter]*
BRUTUS	Come in, Titinius! Welcome, Messala. Gather around the candle and list our needs.
CASSIUS	Portia, are you really gone?
BRUTUS	No more grief, please. Messala, I have learned that Octavius and Mark Antony are leading an army toward Philippi northeast of Greece.
MESSALA	I received the same messages.
BRUTUS	Was there any other news in them?
MESSALA	I learned that Octavius, Antony, and Lepidus have outlawed and executed one hundred senators.
BRUTUS	My message says otherwise. They refer to 70 dead senators, including Cicero.
CASSIUS	Cicero was executed?
MESSALA	Cicero is dead by their orders. Did you also receive letters from Portia, my lord?

ACT IV

TRANSLATION

BRUTUS	No, Messala.
MESSALA	Nor nothing in your letters writ of her?
BRUTUS	Nothing, Messala.
MESSALA	That methinks is strange.
BRUTUS	Why ask you? Hear you aught of her in yours?

185

MESSALA	No, my lord.
BRUTUS	Now as you are a Roman, tell me true.
MESSALA	Then like a Roman bear the truth I tell; For certain she is dead, and by strange manner.

BRUTUS	Why, farewell, Portia. We must die, Messala. With meditating that she must die once, I have the patience to endure it now.

190

MESSALA	Even so great men great losses should endure.
CASSIUS	I have as much of this in art as you, But yet my nature could not bear it so.

195

BRUTUS	Well, to our work alive. What do you think Of marching to Philippi presently?
CASSIUS	I do not think it good.
BRUTUS	Your reason?
CASSIUS	This it is: 'Tis better that the enemy seek us. So shall he waste his means, weary his soldiers, Doing himself offence, whilst we, lying still, Are full of rest, defence, and nimbleness.

200

BRUTUS	Good reasons must of force give place to better. The people 'twixt Philippi and this ground Do stand but in a forced affection; For they have grudged us contribution. The enemy, marching along by them, By them shall make a fuller number up, Come on refreshed, new added, and encouraged; From which advantage shall we cut him off If at Philippi we do face him there, These people at our back.

205

210

CASSIUS	Hear me, good brother.

ORIGINAL

BRUTUS	No, Messala.
MESSALA	Did none of your letters mention her?
BRUTUS	I heard nothing, Messala.
MESSALA	That seems strange.
BRUTUS	Why do you ask? Did you hear anything about her in your letters?
MESSALA	No, my lord.
BRUTUS	On your honor as a patriot, tell me the truth.
MESSALA	Then take my news like a Roman. Portia died by suspicious means.
BRUTUS	Goodbye, Portia. We all must die, Messala. When I concentrate on that fact, I can endure her loss.
MESSALA	You bear your loss like a great man.
CASSIUS	I have as much tolerance as you, but I could not easily bear the loss of Portia.
BRUTUS	Well, the survivors have work to do. What do you think of marching immediately toward Philippi?
CASSIUS	It isn't a good idea.
BRUTUS	Why?
CASSIUS	It would be better for the enemy to look for us. They will waste their supplies, weary their men, and distress themselves while we lie in wait for them and maintain our strength and our defense post.
BRUTUS	My idea is better. The people living between Sardis and Philippi are hostile toward our army. They begrudged contributions to us. The enemy must march through Sardis, where they will add soldiers to their number, take on supplies, and raise morale. It is to our advantage to stop them at Philippi with the people of Sardis behind us.
CASSIUS	Listen to me, Brutus.

ACT IV

BRUTUS	Under your pardon. You must note beside
	That we have tried the utmost of our friends,
	Our legions are brimful, our cause is ripe. 215
	The enemy increaseth every day;
	We, at the height, are ready to decline.
	There is a tide in the affairs of men
	Which, taken at the flood, leads on to fortune;
	Omitted, all the voyage of their life 220
	Is bound in shallows and in miseries.
	On such a full sea are we now afloat,
	And we must take the current when it serves
	Or lose our ventures.
CASSIUS	Then, with your will, go on.
	We'll along ourselves, and meet them at Philippi. 225
BRUTUS	The deep of night is crept upon our talk
	And nature must obey necessity,
	Which we will niggard with a little rest.
	There is no more to say?
CASSIUS	No more. Good night.
	Early to-morrow will we rise and hence. 230
BRUTUS	Lucius! *[Enter LUCIUS]* My gown. *[Exit LUCIUS]*
	Farewell good Messala.
	Good night, Titinius. Noble, noble Cassius,
	Good night and good repose.
CASSIUS	O my dear brother,
	This was an ill beginning of the night! 235
	Never come such division 'tween our souls!
	Let it not, Brutus.
	[Enter LUCIUS with the gown]
BRUTUS	Everything is well.
CASSIUS	Good night, my lord.
BRUTUS	Good night, good brother.
TITINIUS, **MESSALA**	Good night, Lord Brutus.
BRUTUS	Farewell every one.
	[Exeunt CASSIUS, TITINIUS, and MESSALA]
	Give me my gown. Where is thy instrument?
LUCIUS	Here in the tent.

BRUTUS	Let me finish. Note that we have tested our supporters, our legions are full, our cause is just. The enemy grows stronger every day. We are as strong as we will ever be. Human affairs are like the tide. We must sail toward good fortune at the peak. If we don't attack now, our cause will wallow in the backwater. We must sail on a rising sea and follow the current or else lose.
CASSIUS	Then, as you suggest, we will advance to the northwest and meet the enemy at Philippi.
BRUTUS	It is late and we are all tired. Is there anything else to add?
CASSIUS	Nothing. Good night. Early tomorrow we will march toward Philippi.
BRUTUS	Lucius, *[Enter LUCIUS]* bring my nightshirt. *[LUCIUS goes out]* Goodbye, Messala. Goodbye, Titinius. Good night and a good sleep to you, Cassius.
CASSIUS	Dear comrade, this night began in anger! Let's not quarrel like that again, Brutus. *[LUCIUS enters with the gown]*
BRUTUS	Everything is settled.
CASSIUS	Good night, my lord.
BRUTUS	Good night, good comrade.
TITINIUS, MESSALA	Good night, Brutus.
BRUTUS	Goodbye, everyone. *[CASSIUS, TITINIUS, and MESSALA go out]* Give me my nightshirt. Where is your harp?
LUCIUS	Here in the tent.

ACT IV

TRANSLATION

BRUTUS	What, thou speak'st drowsily? 240 Poor knave, I blame thee not; thou art o'erwatched. Call Claudius and some other of my men; I'll have them sleep on cushions in my tent.
LUCIUS	Varro and Claudius! *[Enter VARRO and CLAUDIUS]*
VARRO	Calls my lord? 245
BRUTUS	I pray you, sirs, lie in my tent and sleep. It may be I shall raise you by and by On business to my brother Cassius.
VARRO	So please you, we will stand and watch your pleasure.
BRUTUS	I will not have it so. Lie down, good sirs. 250 It may be I shall otherwise bethink me. *[VARRO and CLAUDIUS lie down]* Look, Lucius, here's the book I sought for so; I put it in the pocket of my gown.
LUCIUS	I was sure your lordship did not give it me.
BRUTUS	Bear with me, good boy, I am much forgetful. 255 Canst thou hold up thy heavy eyes awhile, And touch thy instrument a strain or two?
LUCIUS	Ay, my lord, an't please you.
BRUTUS	It does, my boy. I trouble thee too much, but thou art willing.
LUCIUS	It is my duty, sir. 260
BRUTUS	I should not urge thy duty past thy might. I know young bloods look for a time of rest.
LUCIUS	I have slept, my lord, already.

BRUTUS	You sound sleepy. Poor child, I don't blame you. You have been serving me until late at night. Call Claudius and another soldier to sleep on cushions in my tent.
LUCIUS	Varro and Claudius! *[Enter VARRO and CLAUDIUS]*
VARRO	Did you call, my lord?
BRUTUS	Please, sleep in my tent. I may need to send you to Cassius during the night.
VARRO	If you please, we will stand watch.
BRUTUS	I won't ask you to stay awake. Lie down, sirs. I may change my mind later. *[VARRO and CLAUDIUS lie down]* Look, Lucius, here's the book I was looking for. I put it in my nightshirt pocket.
LUCIUS	I was certain that you didn't give it to me.
BRUTUS	Forgive me, boy, I am forgetful. Can you stay awake long enough to play your harp for me?
LUCIUS	Yes, my lord, if you want.
BRUTUS	I do, my boy. I ask a lot of you, but you are obedient.
LUCIUS	It is my duty, sir.
BRUTUS	I shouldn't put too much strain on you. I know children need their rest.
LUCIUS	I have already slept, my lord.

ACT IV

TRANSLATION

BRUTUS	It was well done; and thou shalt sleep again;
	I will not hold thee long. If I do live, 265
	I will be good to thee.
	[Music, and a song LUCIUS falls asleep]
	This is a sleepy tune. O murd'rous slumber!
	Layest thou thy leaden mace upon my boy,
	That plays thee music? Gentle knave, good night.
	I will not do thee so much wrong to wake thee. 270
	If thou dost nod, thou break'st thy instrument;
	I'll take it from thee; and, good boy, good night.
	Let me see, let me see. Is not the leaf turned down
	Where I left reading? Here it is, I think.
	[Enter the ghost of CAESAR]
	How ill this taper burns! Ha! who comes here? 275
	I think it is the weakness of mine eyes
	That shapes this monstrous apparition.
	It comes upon me. Art thou any thing?
	Art thou some god, some angel, or some devil
	That mak'st my blood cold, and my hair to stare? 280
	Speak to me what thou art.
GHOST	Thy evil spirit, Brutus.
BRUTUS	Why com'st thou?
GHOST	To tell thee thou shalt see me at Philippi.
BRUTUS	Well; then I shall see thee again?
GHOST	Ay, at Philippi. 285
BRUTUS	Why, I will see thee at Philippi then.
	[Exit GHOST]
	Now I have taken heart thou vanishest.
	Ill spirit, I would hold more talk with thee.
	Boy! Lucius! Varro! Sirs! Awake!
	Claudius! 290
LUCIUS	The strings, my lord, are false.
BRUTUS	He thinks he still is at his instrument. Lucius, awake!
LUCIUS	My lord?
BRUTUS	Didst thou dream, Lucius, that thou so criest out?
LUCIUS	My lord, I do not know that I did cry. 295
BRUTUS	Yes, that thou didst. Didst thou see anything?
LUCIUS	Nothing, my lord.

ORIGINAL

BRUTUS	That was wise, and you will soon return to bed. I will not keep you long. If I survive, I will be good to you. *[Music, and a song. LUCIUS falls asleep]* That was a drowsy melody. Oh heavy sleep! Did you carry off my servant while he was playing? Gentle boy, good night. I won't awaken you. If you move, you might break your harp. I will take it from you. Good night, good boy. Let me see. Didn't I turn down a page where I stopped reading? Here it is, I think. *[The ghost of CAESAR enters]* This candle burns unevenly. Who is coming? I think some eye problem makes me see a monstrous vision. It is coming toward me. Are you real? Are you a god, angel, or demon that chills my blood and makes my hair stand up? Tell me what you are.
GHOST	Your bad conscience, Brutus.
BRUTUS	Why are you here?
GHOST	To tell you that you will see me at Philippi.
BRUTUS	Then I will see you again?
GHOST	Yes, at Philippi.
BRUTUS	Well, I will expect to see you at Philippi. *[GHOST departs]* I feel better now that you've vanished. Evil ghost, I want no more visits from you. Boy, Lucius, Varro, sirs, wake up! Claudius!
LUCIUS	My lord, the strings are out of tune.
BRUTUS	He thinks he is still strumming his harp. Lucius, wake up!
LUCIUS	My lord?
BRUTUS	Did a nightmare make you cry out?
LUCIUS	My lord, I didn't know that I was calling.
BRUTUS	Yes, you were. Did you see anything?
LUCIUS	Nothing, my lord.

ACT IV

TRANSLATION

BRUTUS	To sleep again, Lucius. Sirrah Claudius!
	[to VARRO] Fellow thou, awake!
VARRO	My lord? 300
CLAUDIUS	My lord?
BRUTUS	Why did you so cry out, sirs, in your sleep?
BOTH	Did we, my lord?
BRUTUS	Ay. Saw you anything?
VARRO	No, my lord, I saw nothing.
CLAUDIUS	Nor I, my lord. 305
BRUTUS	Go and commend me to my brother Cassius.
	Bid him set on his powers betimes before,
	And we will follow.
BOTH	It shall be done, my lord *[Exeunt]*

BRUTUS	Go back to sleep, Lucius. Claudius. *[to VARRO]* You, there, wake up!
VARRO	My lord?
CLAUDIUS	My lord?
BRUTUS	Why did you call out in your sleep?
BOTH	Did we, my lord?
BRUTUS	Yes. Did you see anything?
VARRO	No, my lord, I saw nothing.
CLAUDIUS	Neither did I, my lord.
BRUTUS	Take a message to Cassius. Have him march ahead of me and my army will follow.
BOTH	We will, my lord. *[They go out]*

TRANSLATION

ACT V, SCENE 1

The Plain of Philippi.

[Enter OCTAVIUS, ANTONY, and their army]

OCTAVIUS	Now, Antony, our hopes are answered.
	You said the enemy would not come down
	But keep the hills and upper regions.
	It proves not so. Their battles are at hand;
	They mean to warn us at Philippi here, 5
	Answering before we do demand of them.
ANTONY	Tut! I am in their bosoms and I know
	Wherefore they do it. They could be content
	To visit other places, and come down
	With fearful bravery, thinking by this face 10
	To fasten in our thoughts that they have courage.
	But 'tis not so.
	[Enter a messenger]
MESSENGER	Prepare you, generals.
	The enemy comes on in gallant show;
	Their bloody sign of battle is hung out,
	And something to be done immediately. 15
ANTONY	Octavius, lead your battle softly on
	Upon the left hand of the even field.
OCTAVIUS	Upon the right hand. Keep thou the left.
ANTONY	Why do you cross me in this exigent?
OCTAVIUS	I do not cross you; but I will do so. 20
	[March. Drum. Enter BRUTUS, CASSIUS, and
	their army, LUCILIUS, TITINIUS, and others]
BRUTUS	They stand and would have parley.
CASSIUS	Stand fast, Titinius. We must out and talk.
OCTAVIUS	Mark Antony, shall we give sign of battle?
ANTONY	No, Caesar, we will answer on their charge.
	Make forth. The generals would have some words. 25
OCTAVIUS	Stir not until the signal.
BRUTUS	Words before blows. Is it so, countrymen?
OCTAVIUS	Not that we love words better, as you do.

ACT V, SCENE 1

The Plain of Philippi.

[Enter OCTAVIUS, ANTONY, and their army]

OCTAVIUS   Antony, this is better than we hoped. You said the enemy would stay entrenched in the slopes, but they are coming this way. They seek a battle at Philippi before we attack them.

ANTONY   I know what they are thinking and why. They would rather be elsewhere. They make a show of courage, thinking to impress us with their bravery. But we aren't fooled. *[Enter a messenger]*

MESSENGER   Get ready. The enemy is making a splendid show of military strength. They wave their battle flag. We must act at once.

ANTONY   Octavius, move slowly to the left.

OCTAVIUS   I want the right. You take the left.

ANTONY   Why are you quibbling during an emergency?

OCTAVIUS   I am not quibbling, but I will do what I want. *[March. Drum. Enter BRUTUS, CASSIUS, and their army, LUCILIUS, TITINIUS, and others]*

BRUTUS   They want a conference.

CASSIUS   Stay put, Titinius. We must meet them for a talk.

OCTAVIUS   Mark Antony, shall we get ready for battle?

ANTONY   No, young Caesar, we will wait until they attack. Let's go and have words with them.

OCTAVIUS   Don't move until I give the signal.

BRUTUS   Talk before fighting. Is this the way you want it, fellow Romans?

OCTAVIUS   Not because we prefer talk to fighting, as you do.

ACT V

TRANSLATION

BRUTUS	Good words are better than bad strokes, Octavius.
ANTONY	In your bad strokes, Brutus, you give good words; 30 Witness the hole you made in Caesar's heart, Crying 'Long live! Hail, Caesar!'
CASSIUS	Antony, The posture of your blows are yet unknown; But for your words, they rob the Hybla bees, And leave them honeyless.
ANTONY	Not stingless too. 35
BRUTUS	O yes, and soundless too! For you have stol'n their buzzing, Antony, And very wisely threat before you sting.
ANTONY	Villains! you did not so when your vile daggers Hacked one another in the sides of Caesar. 40 You showed your teeth like apes, and fawned like hounds, And bowed like bondmen, kissing Caesar's feet; Whilst damned Casca, like a cur, behind Struck Caesar on the neck. O you flatterers!
CASSIUS	Flatterers? Now Brutus, thank yourself! 45 This tongue had not offended so to-day If Cassius might have ruled.
OCTAVIUS	Come, come, the cause! If arguing make us sweat, The proof of it will turn to redder drops. Look, 50 I draw a sword against conspirators. When think you that the sword goes up again? Never, till Caesar's three-and-thirty wounds Be well avenged, or till another Caesar Have added slaughter to the sword of traitors. 55
BRUTUS	Caesar, thou canst not die by traitors' hands Unless thou bring'st them with thee.
OCTAVIUS	So I hope. I was not born to die on Brutus' sword.
BRUTUS	O, if thou wert the noblest of thy strain, Young man, thou couldst not die more honourable. 60
CASSIUS	A peevish schoolboy, worthless of such honour, Joined with a masker and a reveller!
ANTONY	Old Cassius still.

BRUTUS	A conference is better than a battle, Octavius.
ANTONY	In your wrongful attack on Caesar, Brutus, you covered your acts with good words. Look at the hole you cut in Caesar's heart while you proclaimed, "Long live. Hail, Caesar."
CASSIUS	Antony, your style of attack is unknown. Your words are more sugary than the honey of Sicily.
ANTONY	And not without force.
BRUTUS	Yes and groundless. You only buzz, Antony, before you attack.
ANTONY	Traitors, you gave no warning when you hacked into Caesar's body. You grinned like apes, fawned like dogs, and bowed like slaves while you kissed Caesar's feet. While Casca, a damned dog, struck Caesar on the neck from behind. You flatterers!
CASSIUS	Flatterers? Your tongue would not be spouting insults if Cassius were in power.
OCTAVIUS	State your purpose. If we heat our anger, there will be bloodshed. Look, I draw my sword against the conspirators. When do you think I will stop fighting? Not until I have avenged the 33 stab wounds on Caesar's body or until you traitors have killed another Caesar.
BRUTUS	Young Caesar, you can't be killed by traitors until you join your army.
OCTAVIUS	That is what I hope. I don't intend to let Brutus kill me.
BRUTUS	If you were the noblest of your family, young man, you couldn't die more honorably than Julius Caesar did.
CASSIUS	A whiny schoolboy, undeserving of honor, along with a deceiver and a carouser!
ANTONY	The same old Cassius.

ACT V

TRANSLATION

OCTAVIUS	Come, Antony, away!
	Defiance, traitors, hurl we in your teeth.
	If you dare fight to-day, come to the fields; 65
	If not, when you have stomachs.
	[Exeunt OCTAVIUS, ANTONY, and army]
CASSIUS	Why now blow wind, swell billow, and swim bark!
	The storm is up, and all is on the hazard.
BRUTUS	Ho, Lucilius! Hark, a word with you.
LUCILIUS	My lord?
	[BRUTUS and LUCILIUS talk apart]
CASSIUS	Messala.
MESSALA	What says my general?
CASSIUS	Messala, 70
	This is my birthday; as this very day
	Was Cassius born. Give me thy hand, Messala.
	Be thou my witness that against my will
	(As Pompey was) am I compelled to set
	Upon one battle all our liberties. 75
	You know that I held Epicurus strong
	And his opinion. Now I change my mind
	And partly credit things that do presage.
	Coming from Sardis, on our former ensign
	Two mighty eagles fell; and there they perched, 80
	Gorging and feeding from our soldiers' hands,
	Who to Philippi here consorted us.
	This morning they are fled away and gone,
	And in their steads do ravens, crows, and kites
	Fly o'er our heads and downward look on us 85
	As we were sickly prey. Their shadows seem
	A canopy most fatal, under which
	Our army lies, ready to give up the ghost.
MESSALA	Believe not so.
CASSIUS	I but believe it partly;
	For I am fresh of spirit and resolved 90
	To meet all perils very constantly.
BRUTUS	Even so Lucilius.

OCTAVIUS	Let's go, Antony. We challenge you traitors. If you want a battle today, come to the field. If you don't, come when you feel more like fighting. *[OCTAVIUS, ANTONY, and the army depart]*
CASSIUS	Let the wind blow and the boat sail. The tempest has risen and everything is at stake.
BRUTUS	Lucilius, I want a word with you.
LUCILIUS	My Lord? *[BRUTUS and LUCILIUS talk apart]*
CASSIUS	Messala.
MESSALA	What do you want, sir?
CASSIUS	Messala, today is my birthday. Shake my hand, Messala. Witness that I must fight against my will (as Pompey did) and that I risk all our freedoms. You know that I admire the philosophy of Epicurus, a realist. I have changed my mind about realism in part because of omens. On the sail from Sardis, two eagles perched on our banner and ate out of the hands of the soldiers who accompanied us. This morning, the eagles were gone. In their place came black birds and scavengers that flew over us as though we were dead meat for them to feed on. Their shadows seemed ominous, as though our armies were doomed.
MESSALA	Don't think gloomy thoughts.
CASSIUS	I only partly believe it. My spirit is renewed and determined to face danger.
BRUTUS	So it is, Lucilius.

ACT V

TRANSLATION

CASSIUS
                           Now, most noble Brutus,
The gods to-day stand friendly, that we may,
Lovers in peace, lead on our days to age!
But since the affairs of men rest still uncertain,   95
Let's reason with the worst that may befall.
If we do lose this battle, then is this
The very last time we shall speak together.
What are you then determined to do?

BRUTUS
Even by the rule of that philosophy   100
By which I did blame Cato for the death
Which he did give himself—I know not how,
But I do find it cowardly and vile,
For fear of what might fall, so to prevent
The time of life—arming myself with patience   105
To stay the providence of some high powers
That govern us below.

CASSIUS
                              Then, if we lose this battle,
You are contented to be led in triumph
Through the streets of Rome?

BRUTUS
No, Cassius, no. Think not, thou noble Roman,   110
That ever Brutus will go bound to Rome.
He bears too great a mind. But this same day
Must end that work the ides of March begun,
And whether we shall meet again I know not.
Therefore our everlasting farewell take.   115
For ever and for ever farewell, Cassius!
If we do meet again, why, we shall smile;
If not, why then this parting was well made.

CASSIUS
For ever and for ever farewell, Brutus!
If we do meet again, we'll smile indeed;   120
If not, 'tis true this parting was well made.

BRUTUS
Why then, lead on. O that a man might know
The end of this day's business ere it come!
But it sufficeth that the day will end,
And then the end is known. Come, ho! Away!   125
[Exeunt]

CASSIUS	Brutus, the gods smile on us today that we may survive and live to old age in peace. But since human life is precarious, let's determine the worst that can happen. If we lose and never talk again, what do you plan to do?
BRUTUS	I reject suicide, a choice that caused me to denounce Cato for killing himself. I think suicide is vile and cowardly by fearing what will happen and wasting part of life. I plan to be patient and await the judgment of those in power.
CASSIUS	Then if we lose, you will allow yourself to be marched in their victory parade through Rome.
BRUTUS	No, Cassius. I would never let myself be displayed in Rome as a prisoner of war. I am too proud for disgrace. We must end the work we began on March 15. I don't know whether we will ever meet again. Let's say our goodbyes now. Forever, farewell, Cassius. If we do survive, we will smile at our goodbyes. If not, then this is a good time to part permanently.
CASSIUS	Forever, goodbye, Brutus! If we do survive, we will certainly smile. If not, then this was a worthy parting.
BRUTUS	March on. I wish I could know the outcome of this battle! But it is enough to know that the day will end and the outcome will be decided. Let's go. *[They depart]*

ACT V

ACT V, SCENE 2

The battlefield.

[Alarum. Enter BRUTUS and MESSALA]

BRUTUS   Ride, ride, Messala, ride, and give these bills
Unto the legions on the other side. *[Loud alarum]*
Let them set on at once; for I perceive
But cold demeanour in Octavius' wing,
And sudden push gives them the overthrow.   5
Ride, ride, Messala! Let them all come down.
[Exeunt]

ACT V, SCENE 2

The battlefield.

[A trumpet call. BRUTUS and MESSALA enter]

BRUTUS Ride on, Messala, and take these orders to the legions on
the opposite side of the battlefield. *[Loud trumpet call]*
Have them to attack at once. I see that Octavius' forces
are spiritless. A sudden attack may trounce them.
Ride, Messala! Send our forces down from the hill.
[They depart]

ACT V, SCENE 3

The battlefield.

[Alarum. Enter CASSIUS and TITINIUS]

CASSIUS	O look, Titinius, look! The villains fly!
	Myself have to mine own turned enemy.
	This ensign here of mine was turning back;
	I slew the coward and did take it from him.
TITINIUS	O Cassius, Brutus gave the word too early, 5
	Who, having some advantage on Octavius,
	Took it too eagerly. His soldiers fell to spoil,
	Whilst we by Antony are all enclosed.
	[Enter PINDARUS]
PINDARUS	Fly further off, my lord! Fly further off!
	Mark Antony is in your tents, my lord. 10
	Fly therefore, noble Cassius, fly far off!
CASSIUS	This hill is far enough. Look, look, Titinius!
	Are those my tents where I perceive the fire?
TITINIUS	They are, my lord.
CASSIUS	Titinius, if thou lovest me,
	Mount thou my horse and hide thy spurs in him 15
	Till he have brought thee up to yonder troops
	And here again, that I may rest assured
	Whether yond troops are friend or enemy.
TITINIUS	I will be here again even with a thought. *[Exit]*
CASSIUS	Go, Pindarus, get higher on that hill. 20
	My sight was ever thick. Regard Titinius,
	And tell me what thou not'st about the field.
	[PINDARUS goes up]
	This day I breathed first. Time is come round,
	And where I did begin, there shall I end.
	My life is run his compass. Sirrah, what news? 25
PINDARUS	*[Above]* O my lord!
CASSIUS	What news?

ACT V, SCENE 3

The battlefield.

[A trumpet call. CASSIUS and TITINIUS enter]

CASSIUS   Look, Titinius! My own men are retreating! I denounce my troops. My flag bearer retreated. I killed him and took the banner from him.

TITINIUS   Oh Cassius, Brutus advanced too soon. He was too eager to seize the advantage against Octavius. His army began looting while we were surrounded by Antony's forces. *[Enter PINDARUS]*

PINDARUS   Ride further away, my lord. Mark Antony has seized your tents.

CASSIUS   This hill is far enough away. Look, Titinius! Are those my tents that are on fire?

TITINIUS   Yes, my lord.

CASSIUS   Titinius, if you are loyal, take my horse and spur him toward those distant troops. Return and report whether those warriors are ours or the enemy's.

TITINIUS   I will return in a second. *[He goes out]*

CASSIUS   Pindarus, climb that hill. My view is obscured. Investigate, Titinius, and describe the battlefield. *[PINDARUS climbs the hill]* Today on my birthday, I will die. My life is over. Sir, what can you report?

PINDARUS   *[Above]* Oh my lord!

CASSIUS   What is happening?

ACT V

PINDARUS	*[Above]* Titinius is enclosed round about
	With horsemen that make to him on the spur.
	Yet he spurs on. Now they are almost on him. 30
	Now Titinius! Now some light. O, he lights too!
	He's ta'en. *[Shout]* And hark! They shout for joy.
CASSIUS	Come down; behold no more.
	O coward that I am to live so long
	To see my best friend ta'en before my face! 35
	[Enter PINDARUS from above]
	Come hither, sirrah.
	In Parthia did I take thee prisoner;
	And then I swore thee, saving of thy life,
	That whatsoever I did bid thee do,
	Thou shouldst attempt it. Come now, keep thine oath. 40
	Now be a freeman, and with this good sword,
	That ran through Caesar's bowels, search this bosom.
	Stand not to answer. Here, take thou the hilts;
	And when my face is covered, as 'tis now,
	Guide thou the sword.
	[PINDARUS stabs him]
	Caesar thou art revenged 45
	Even with the sword that killed thee. *[Dies]*
PINDARUS	So, I am free; yet would not so have been,
	Durst I have done my will. O Cassius!
	Far from this country Pindarus shall run,
	Where never Roman shall take note of him. *[Exit]* 50
	[Enter TITINIUS and MESSALA]
MESSALA	It is but change, Titinius for Octavius
	Is overthrown by noble Brutus' power,
	As Cassius' legions are by Antony.
TITINIUS	These tidings will well comfort Cassius.
MESSALA	Where did you leave him?
TITINIUS	All disconsolate, 55
	With Pindarus his bondman, on this hill.
MESSALA	Is not that he that lies upon the ground?
TITINIUS	He lies not like the living. O my heart!
MESSALA	Is not that he?

PINDARUS	*[Above]* Cavalry surrounded Titinius. He rides on. Some alight from their horses. Titinius also gets off. He is captured. *[A shout from the field]* Oh, listen, the enemy shouts for joy.
CASSIUS	Come back, Pindarus. Don't look at any more of the battle. I am a coward for having lived long enough to see my comrade captured before my eyes! *[Enter PINDARUS from above]* Come here, Pindarus. I took you prisoner in Parthia in western Turkey. I made you swear that, for saving your life, you would do whatever I asked. Keep your promise. You may go free if you pierce my chest with the sword that stabbed Caesar. Don't answer me. Take the hilt. When I cover my face, strike me with the sword. *[PINDARUS stabs Cassius]* Caesar, your death is avenged with the same sword that killed you. *[Cassius dies]*
PINDARUS	I am a free man, but I would have chosen to disobey you. Oh Cassius! I will flee far from Philippi where there are no Romans to see me. *[He goes out]* *[Enter TITINIUS and MESSALA]*
MESSALA	There is no victory—Brutus defeated Octavius; Antony defeated Cassius.
TITINIUS	Cassius will be glad to hear the news.
MESSALA	Where was he when you left?
TITINIUS	He stood depressed on the hill with his slave Pindarus.
MESSALA	Isn't that Cassius on the ground?
TITINIUS	He looks like a corpse. Oh no!
MESSALA	Isn't that Cassius?

ACT V

TITINIUS   No, this was he, Messala,
But Cassius is no more. O setting sun,   60
As in thy red rays thou dost sink to night,
So in his red blood Cassius' day is set!
The sun of Rome is set. Our day is gone;
Clouds, dews, and dangers come; our deeds are done!
Mistrust of my success hath done this deed.   65

MESSALA   Mistrust of good success hath done this deed.
O hateful Error, Melancholy's child,
Why dost thou show to the apt thoughts of men
The things that are not? O Error, soon conceived,
Thou never com'st unto a happy birth,   70
But kill'st the mother that engendered thee!

TITINIUS   What, Pindarus! Where art thou, Pindarus?

MESSALA   Seek him, Titinius whilst I go to meet
The noble Brutus, thrusting this report
Into his ears. I may say 'thrusting' it,   75
For piercing steel and darts envenomed
Shall be as welcome to the ears of Brutus
As tidings of this sight.

TITINIUS   Hie you, Messala,
And I will seek for Pindarus the while.
[Exit MESSALA]
Why didst thou send me forth, brave Cassius?   80
Did I not meet thy friends, and did not they
Put on my brows this wreath of victory
And bid me give it thee? Didst thou not hear their shouts?
Alas, thou has misconstrued everything!
But hold thee, take this garland on thy brow.   85
Thy Brutus bid me give it thee, and I
Will do his bidding. Brutus, come apace
And see how I regarded Caius Cassius.
By your leave, gods, This is a Roman's part.
Come, Cassius' sword, and find Titinius' heart.   90
[Stabs himself and dies]
[Alarum. Enter BRUTUS, MESSALA, YOUNG CATO,
STRATO, VOLUMNIUS, and LUCILIUS]

BRUTUS   Where, where, Messala, doth his body lie?

MESSALA   Lo, yonder, and Titinius mourning it.

BRUTUS   Titinius face is upward.

CATO   He is slain.

TITINIUS	Messala, Cassius is dead. The setting sun is red like that blood that ended Cassius' last day! Rome's power is gone. Our rule is gone. Our actions end with clouds, tears, and danger. Lack of trust in my mission caused Cassius to kill himself.
MESSALA	Doubts about victory caused Cassius to die. Oh what a miserable mistake. Why did Cassius mistake a victory for a defeat? A mistake that caused Cassius' suicide.
TITINIUS	Pindarus, where are you?
MESSALA	Find him, Titinius, while I report to Brutus what has happened. My news will hurt Brutus like an arrow through his armor.
TITINIUS	Hurry, Messala, while I look for Pindarus. *[MESSALA goes out]* Why did you send me on a mission, Cassius? Didn't I join your troops? Didn't they decorate me with the victory wreath and ask me to bring it to you? Didn't you hear their shouts? You misunderstood! Wear on your head this victory wreath that Brutus sent you. I will do as he asked. Brutus, hurry and see the honor I placed on Caius Cassius. With your permission, gods, I will die like a Roman by thrusting Cassius' sword into my chest. *[He stabs himself and dies] [A trumpet sounds. Entering are BRUTUS, MESSALA, YOUNG CATO, STRATO, VOLUMNIUS, and LUCILIUS]*

ACT V

BRUTUS	Messala, where is Cassius' body?
MESSALA	Look there, where Titinius mourns him.
BRUTUS	Titinius is lying on his back.
CATO	He is dead.

BRUTUS   O Julius Caesar, thou art mighty yet!
                    Thy spirit walks abroad and turns our swords   95
                    In our own proper entrails. *[Low alarums]*

CATO   Brave Titinius!
                    Look whe'r he have not crowned dead Cassius.

BRUTUS   Are yet two Romans living such as these?
                    The last of all the Romans, fare thee well!
                    It is impossible that ever Rome   100
                    Should breed thy fellow. Friends, I owe moe tears
                    To this dead man than you shall see me pay.
                    I shall find time, Cassius; I shall find time.
                    Come therefore, and to Thasos send his body.
                    His funerals shall not be in our camps,   105
                    Lest it discomfort us. Lucilius, come;
                    And come, young Cato. Let us to the field.
                    Labeo and Flavius set our battles on
                    'Tis three o'clock; and, Romans, yet ere night
                    We shall try fortune in a second fight. *[Exeunt]*   110

BRUTUS	Oh Julius Caesar, you are still powerful! Your ghost haunts us here and causes us to kill ourselves. *[Muffled trumpet calls]*
CATO	Brave Titinius! He crowned Cassius' corpse.
BRUTUS	Are there any living Romans as fine as these men? The last of the true patriots, farewell! Rome shall never produce the equals of these men. Friends, I owe Cassius more tears than I can weep. I will find time to mourn you, Cassius. Send his body to Thasos, an island south of here. We won't hold his funeral in camp because it will depress us. Lucilius and young Cato, let us return to the battlefield. Labeo and Flavius are leading our forces in combat. It's 3:00 p.m. Before night, Romans, we will try our luck in another attack. *[They go out]*

ACT V, SCENE 4

The battlefield.

[Alarum. Enter BRUTUS, MESSALA, YOUNG CATO, LUCILIUS, and FLAVIUS]

BRUTUS　　Yet, countrymen, O yet hold up your heads!
[Exit BRUTUS, MESSALA, and FLAVIUS]

CATO　　What bastard doth not? Who will go with me?
I will proclaim my name about the field.
I am the son of Marcus Cato, ho!
A foe to tyrants, and my country's friend.　　　　　5
I am the son of Marcus Cato, ho!
[Enter soldiers and fight]

LUCILIUS　　And I am Brutus, Marcus Brutus I!
Brutus, my country's friend! Know me for Brutus!
[YOUNG CATO falls]
O young and noble Cato, art thou down?
Why, now thou diest as bravely as Titinius,　　　10
And may'st be honoured, being Cato's son.

1ST SOLDIER　　Yield, or thou diest.

LUCILIUS　　　　　　　　　　Only I yield to die.
There is so much that thou wilt kill me straight.
Kill Brutus, and be honoured in his death.

1ST SOLDIER　　We must not. A noble prisoner!　　　　15
[Enter ANTONY]

2ND SOLDIER　　Room ho! Tell Antony Brutus is ta'en.

1ST SOLDIER　　I'll tell the news. Here comes the general.
Brutus is ta'en! Brutus is ta'en, my lord!

ANTONY　　Where is he?

LUCILIUS　　Safe, Antony; Brutus is safe enough.　　　20
I dare assure thee that no enemy
Shall ever take alive the noble Brutus.
The gods defend him from so great a shame!
When you do find him, or alive or dead,
He will be found like Brutus, like himself.　　　25

ACT V, SCENE 4

The battlefield.

[A trumpet sounds. Entering are BRUTUS, MESSALA, YOUNG CATO, LUCILIUS, and FLAVIUS]

BRUTUS   Fellow Romans, hold up your heads with pride! *[BRUTUS, MESSALA, and FLAVIUS depart]*

CATO   What bastard refuses to fight? Who will go into battle with me? Who will shout my name on the battlefield? I am the son of Marcus Cato. I denounce tyrants and support my country. I am Marcus Cato's son. *[Enter soldiers and fight]*

LUCILIUS   I am Brutus, Marcus Brutus! I am a patriot. *[YOUNG CATO dies in battle]* Oh young and noble Cato, are you killed? I am Brutus, the patriot! You died as bravely as Titinius. You deserve honor, young Cato.

1ST SOLDIER   Surrender or die.

LUCILIUS   I surrender only in death. You must kill me instantly. Kill Brutus and earn yourself honor.

1ST SOLDIER   We must not kill him. He is a valuable prisoner of war! *[Enter ANTONY]*

2ND SOLDIER   Stand back. Report to Antony that we have captured Brutus.

1ST SOLDIER   I will report to Antony. Here he comes. We have captured Brutus, my lord!

ANTONY   Where is he.

LUCILIUS   He is safe, Antony. I promise you that no enemy will take Brutus alive. The Gods defend him from shame! When you find him, alive or dead, he will still be Brutus.

ANTONY   This is not Brutus, friend; but, I assure you,
          A prize no less in worth. Keep this man safe;
          Give him all kindness. I had rather have
          Such men my friends than enemies. Go on,
          And see whe'r Brutus be alive or dead;   30
          And bring us word unto Octavius' tent
          How every thing is chanced. *[Exeunt]*

ORIGINAL

ANTONY   This is not Brutus. I promise you that Lucilius is still a prize worth having. Keep Lucilius safe and treat him well. I would rather have a man like him for a friend than for an enemy. Continue the search for Brutus. Report what you find to me at Octavius' tent. *[They depart]*

TRANSLATION

ACT V, SCENE 5

The battlefield.

[Enter BRUTUS, DARDANIUS, CLITUS, STRATO, and VOLUMNIUS]

BRUTUS	Come, poor remains of friends, rest on this rock.
CLITUS	Statilius showed the torchlight; but my lord, He came not back. He is or ta'en or slain.
BRUTUS	Sit thee down, Clitus. Slaying is the word. It is a deed in fashion. Hark thee, Clitus. *[Whispers]*
CLITUS	What, I, my lord? No, not for all the world!
BRUTUS	Peace then. No words.
CLITUS	I'll rather kill myself.
BRUTUS	Hark thee, Dardanius. *[Whispers]*
DARDANIUS	Shall I do such a deed?
CLITUS	O Dardanius!
DARDANIUS	O Clitus!
CLITUS	What ill request did Brutus make to thee?
DARDANIUS	To kill him, Clitus. Look, he meditates.
CLITUS	Now is that noble vessel full of grief, That it runs over even at his eyes.
BRUTUS	Come hither, good Volumnius. List a word.
VOLUMNIUS	What says my lord?
BRUTUS	Why this, Volumnius. The ghost of Caesar hath appeared to me Two several times by night—at Sardis once, And this last night here in Philippi fields. I know my hour is come.
VOLUMNIUS	Not so, my lord.

5

10

15

20

ACT V, SCENE 5

The battlefield.

[Enter BRUTUS, DARDANIUS, CLITUS, STRATO, and VOLUMNIUS]

BRUTUS	My surviving friends, let's rest on this rock.
CLITUS	Statilius signaled with a torch, but he didn't return. He is either captured or dead.
BRUTUS	Sit down here, Clitus. There is too much killing here. Listen to me, Clitus. *[BRUTUS whispers to CLITUS]*
CLITUS	I, my lord? I wouldn't do it for anything!
BRUTUS	Quiet, then. Say nothing.
CLITUS	I would rather kill myself.
BRUTUS	Listen, Dardanius. *[BRUTUS whispers to DARDANIUS]*
DARDANIUS	Could I do such a thing?
CLITUS	Oh Dardanius!
DARDANIUS	Oh Clitus!
CLITUS	What disturbing request did Brutus ask of you?
DARDANIUS	To kill him, Clitus. See, he is thinking.
CLITUS	He is so filled with sorrow that he weeps.
BRUTUS	Come here, good Volumnius. Listen to me.
VOLUMNIUS	What is it, my lord?
BRUTUS	Volumnius, Caesar's ghost has appeared to me on two nights—once at Sardis and last night here at Philippi. I know that I will die.
VOLUMNIUS	No, my lord.

BRUTUS	Nay, I am sure it is, Volumnius.
	Thou seest the world, Volumnius, how it goes.
	Our enemies have beat us to the pit.
	[Low alarums]
	It is more worthy to leap in ourselves
	Than tarry till they push us. Good Volumnius, 25
	Thou know'st that we two went to school together.
	Even for that our love of old, I prithee
	Hold thou my sword-hilts whilst I run on it.
VOLUMNIUS	That's not an office for a friend, my lord. *[Alarums still]*
CLITUS	Fly, fly, my lord! There is no tarrying here. 30
BRUTUS	Farewell to you; and you; and you, Volumnius.
	Strato, thou hast been all this while asleep.
	Farewell to thee too, Strato. Countrymen,
	My heart doth joy that yet in all my life
	I found no man but he was true to me. 35
	I shall have glory by this losing day
	More than Octavius and Mark Antony
	By this vile conquest shall attain unto.
	So fare you well at once; for Brutus' tongue
	Hath almost ended his life's history. 40
	Night hangs upon mine eyes; my bones would rest,
	That have but laboured to attain this hour.
	[Alarum. Cry within 'Fly, fly, fly!']
CLITUS	Fly, my lord, fly!
BRUTUS	Hence! I will follow.
	[Exeunt CLITUS, DARDANIUS, and VOLUMNIUS]
	I prithee, Strato, stay thou by thy lord.
	Thou art a fellow of a good respect;
	Thy life hath had some smatch of honour in it. 45
	Hold then my sword, and turn away thy face
	While I do run upon it. Wilt thou, Strato?
STRATO	Give me your hand first. Fare you well, my lord.
BRUTUS	Farewell, good Strato. *[Runs on his sword]*
	Caesar, now be still. 50
	I killed not thee with half so good a will. *[Dies]*
	[Alarum. Retreat. Enter OCTAVIUS, ANTONY,
	MESSALA, LUCILIUS, and the army]
OCTAVIUS	What man is that?
MESSALA	My master's man. Strato, where is thy master?

BRUTUS	I am certain I will die, Volumnius. You see the situation, Volumnius. Our enemies are winning. *[Distant trumpets]* It is more honorable to kill ourselves than to wait to be killed. Volumnius, we were schoolmates. For our long friendship, I beg that you hold my sword while I run against it.
VOLUMNIUS	That is not something a friend would do, my lord. *[Trumpet calls continue]*
CLITUS	Run, my lord, don't stay here!
BRUTUS	Goodbye to you and to Volumnius. Strato, you have been sleeping. Goodbye, Strato. I am pleased that, all my life, I have found trusted friends. I shall have victory in this loss more than either Octavius or Mark Antony shall have from conquering us. Goodbye. I have finished my life history. Death hangs over my eyes. My bones are weary. They have toiled to reach this hour. *[A trumpet call. A cry within, "Run, run, run!"]*
CLITUS	Hurry, my lord!
BRUTUS	Go on. I will follow. *[CLITUS, DARDANIUS, and VOLUMNIUS depart]* Please, Strato. Stay with your master. You are a respectable man. Your life has known a touch of honor. Hold my sword and turn your head while I run on the point. Will you do it, Strato?
STRATO	Shake my hand first. Goodbye, my lord.
BRUTUS	Farewell, good Strato. *[BRUTUS runs against his sword]* Caesar, be at peace. I killed myself much more willingly than I killed you. *[BRUTUS dies] [A trumpet sounds retreat. Entering are OCTAVIUS, ANTONY, MESSALA, LUCILIUS, and the army]*
OCTAVIUS	Who is this?
MESSALA	My master's servant. Strato, where is Brutus?

ACT V

STRATO	Free from the bondage you are in Messala.
	The conquerors can but make a fire of him;	55
	For Brutus only overcame himself,
	And no man else hath honour by his death.

| LUCILIUS | So Brutus should be found. I thank thee, Brutus, |
| | That thou hast proved Lucilius' saying true. |

| OCTAVIUS | All that served Brutus, I will entertain them. | 60 |
| | Fellow, wilt thou bestow thy time with me? |

| STRATO | Ay, if Messala will prefer me to you. |

| OCTAVIUS | Do so, good Messala. |

| MESSALA | How died my master, Strato? |

| STRATO | I held the sword, and he did run on it. | 65 |

| MESSALA | Octavius, then take him to follow thee, |
| | That did the latest service to my master. |

ANTONY	This was the noblest Roman of them all.
	All the conspirators save only he
	Did what they did in envy of great Caesar;	70
	He only, in a general honest thought
	And common good to all, made one of them.
	His life was gentle, and the elements
	So mixed in him that Nature might stand up
	And say to all the world, 'This was a man!'	75

OCTAVIUS	According to his virtue let us use him,
	With all respect and rites of burial.
	Within my tent his bones to-night shall lie,
	Most like a soldier, ordered honourably.
	So call the field to rest, and let's away	80
	To part the glories of this happy day. *[Exeunt]*

STRATO	Free from the life that holds you, Messala. The victors can burn his body. Brutus killed himself. No one else can claim that honor.
LUCILIUS	Find Brutus' body. I thank you, Brutus, for proving my claim.
OCTAVIUS	I will employ all of Brutus' staff. Fellow, will you serve me?
STRATO	Yes, if Messala gives me a recommendation.
OCTAVIUS	Do so, Messala.
MESSALA	How did Brutus die, Strato?
STRATO	I held his sword and he ran against it.
MESSALA	Octavius, take Strato as a servant. He served my master to the end.
ANTONY	This was the noblest Roman among the conspirators. All the other killers envied Caesar. Only he joined the conspiracy for the good of Rome's citizens. He was a gentleman. His qualities were so balanced that nature might call him a man.
OCTAVIUS	Because of his good character, let us respect him with a proper burial. His remains will lie in state in my tent tonight, honorably, like a soldier. End the battle and let us share the victory. *[They go out]*

ACT V

Questions for Reflection

1. How does Shakespeare adapt the tragedy of Julius Caesar to the Elizabethan stage? How do the victory parade, the stormy night, domestic discussions between husbands and wives, a ghostly apparition, and the battle scene suit inner and outer portions of the Globe Theater?

2. How does Shakespeare indicate that the death of Julius Caesar leaves vulnerable an array of people, including Publius, Cicero, and Cinna the poet? Consider the gloom and depression that engulf Portia, Cassius, and Brutus. Why does young Cato claim to be the son of Marcus Cato? Why does Cato the elder require defense? Why is Portia proud to be Cato's daughter?

3. Which lines from the play reveal superstition about birds, weather, dreams, ritual, and corpses? How does the custom at the foot race affect Caesar's concern for Calpurnia's childlessness? Explain why Cassius changes his low opinion of Roman bird lore.

4. How do Caesar, Pompey, Cassius, Brutus, Lepidus, Mark Antony, and Octavius compare as leaders? Note which characters die ignobly and which cling to nobility and patriotism.

5. How would you describe the theme of loyalty as it applies to these pairs: Casca/Cassius, Mark Antony/Caesar, Lucius/Brutus, Pindarus/Cassius, Mark Antony/Lepidus, Lucilius/Brutus, Cicero/Caesar, Artemidorus/Caesar, Brutus/Portia, and Strato/Brutus?

6. Why does Caesar remain a force within the play until Act V? Why would English playgoers believe in ghostly visitations?

7. What forms of dishonesty occur during the play? Consider forged letters, manipulation of conspirators, and sniping behind Lepidus' back. How does Mark Antony mislead the mob while pointing out stab wounds on Caesar's cloak and on his body? Where was Mark Antony the day that Caesar defeated the Nervii? Why would a soldier claim to be Brutus?

8. How does Shakespeare present the causes and symptoms of tyranny? Why do Romans appear to love Caesar even though he is a tyrant?

9. What strengths does Brutus have that Cassius lacks? Why does Portia admire her husband during his period of unrest? How does Brutus' treatment of Lucius and Strato affirm Shakespeare's treatment of Brutus as a fallen hero? Why does Octavius honor Brutus?

10. Why is Brutus unwise to let Mark Antony speak second at the public lectern? How does Mark Antony turn Brutus' speech against him? Consider the examples of repetition, irony, rhetorical question, understatement, caesura, and alliteration found in Mark Antony's speech.

11. How would you summarize the play's presentation of civil war? Why is Brutus naive to think that one murder will restore Rome to proper rule and order? How far from Rome does the civil war advance? Why is Pindarus wise to slip away?

12. How do you account for Mark Antony's false modesty that he is not so gifted a speaker as Brutus? What does Mark Antony reveal about himself in his three most emotional speeches—his address to Caesar's corpse, the funeral oration, and his eulogy for Brutus?

13. How does the silencing of Marullus and Flavius substantiate Cassius' claim that Caesar is too powerful? Why do the two tribunes insist on loyalty to Pompey?

14. At what point does Octavius adopt the name "Caesar"? Locate in Octavius' few comments evidence of the great leader he becomes as Rome's first emperor.

15. How does Shakespeare use light and dark as symbols of good and evil? Why is lightning ominous to Brutus the night before the assassination? Why do the conspirators lurk about Pompey's porch and conceal their faces? What do Portia and Lucius think about their behaviors?

16. What are the patriotic qualities of Julius Caesar, Mark Antony, Cassius, Octavius, and Brutus? Which is most sincere? Most manipulative? Most self-serving?

17. How would you summarize the role of the mob as a source of retribution, morality, and disorder? What happens to the mob's commitment when it has no leader to follow?

18. How would you explain the use of the following details as evidence of vengeance: murder weapons, rioting and arson, street murder, oaths, striking from behind, a list of people to be executed, a ghost, a flickering candle, burning tents, and multiple suicides?

19. What is the situation in Sardis when Brutus and Cassius bivouac their armies there? Why does Brutus insist on sailing to Philippi? What are his reasons for overruling Cassius?

20. How would you define political expedience? Use as models Octavius' pause before entering Rome, Julius Caesar's refusal of a crown, an apology for an epileptic seizure, Mark Antony's use of a funeral speech to turn Romans against the assassins, and a plot to cheat Caesar's heirs.

21. How would you summarize two interpretations of Calpurnia's dream? Propose other interpretations that offer extremes of prophecy.

22. How does each death bring down the conspiracy? Why does Cassius choose to die on his birthday?

23. How would you define Gothic convention using examples from the stormy night, the disclosure of stab wounds, blood on Pompey's statue, Portia's wounded thigh, ritual sacrifice and the search for a heart, military suicide, swallowing hot coals, open graves, ravens and kites, and two appearances of a ghost?

24. Why does the argument between Brutus and Cassius require skillful acting? Why does Brutus lie to Messala about letters from Portia?

25. How does Shakespeare provide multiple views of Cassius' personality? Consider how the character changes from the opening scene to his suicide. Why is he ill-matched with Brutus?

26. How would you explain the confusion regarding the order for the troops to sweep down from the hill against the enemy? How might uniforms or better forms of communication have spared the losing side from so much death?

27. What does Shakespeare imply about the cause and spread of tyranny? How does the patriotism of Lucius Junius Brutus set the tone for noble, but dangerous deeds?

28. How does the last act typify human failing? What aspects of military suicide force accomplices into slaughter? How does suicide leave slaves in jeopardy?

29. In what way is Lepidus like a horse? What does the simile reveal about Shakespeare's use of animal imagery? Of incongruity? Of hyperbole? Of incidental humor?

30. How does Shakespeare place demands on his audience? What would English playgoers need to know about Roman history to appreciate the play—for example, the identity of the "threefold world," Pompey, Cato, and Cicero? What does the play suggest about the stability of a triumvirate?

31. Which lines would you cite that attest to weakness in Julius Caesar? For example, consider the deafness in his left ear, his failure to swim the distance, his love of flatterers, his acquiescence to Calpurnia's demands, and his thirst from the fever he contracted in Spain.

32. How does Portia describe the role of most Roman wives? How does her relationship with Brutus differ from the ordinary marriage? How does she justify her role as a noble wife? How does Cassius honor her?

33. Which characters appeal to players of bit parts? Which speeches reveal nobility, wit, vulnerability, humor, survivalism, loyalty, and humanity? What kind of actor would best play the roles of Peblius, Lucius, Portia, Artemidorus, Strato, Metellus Cimber, and Pindarus?

34. How would you contrast the qualities that Mark Antony describes in his funeral oration with historical evidence of Julius Caesar's life and behavior? Why was Julius Caesar admired for leadership, political savvy, concern for commoners, oratory, charisma, and courage? What evidence proves that he was a tyrant and schemer?

35. How does the riot after the funeral compare with the battle at Philippi? Which event best expresses Roman patriotism?

36. Why does the play open with witty remarks from working Romans? Why does Shakespeare describe the Romans as fickle and undeserving of committed leadership? Why do citizens propose elevating Brutus to Caesar's former office?

37. Why does Shakespeare predict that the death of Julius Caesar will one day be acted on the stage? Was he referring only to his play?

38. How does Shakespeare use irony in the final act? What does Brutus suffer by rejecting Cassius' advice? Why do honors to Brutus come too late for him to appreciate them?

39. Summarize the use of gentle and innocent characters to balance belligerent players. Consider Lucius, Cinna the Poet, Calpurnia, and Portia.

40. Explain why the play refers to absent characters. How do these Romans influence actions: Cato, Pompey, the standard-bearer, Brutus' ancestor, Cicero, Tarquin, Auguers, Publius Cimber, and Mark Antony's nephew?

41. Construct family trees of related characters. Include Portia, Cassius, Brutus, Cato, and Brutus' ancestor. Make a separate tree for Julius Caesar, Calpurnia, Octavius, and Pompey. Where does Mark Antony belong on the second tree?

42. Account for obvious anachronisms, particularly hats pulled down, open doublets, and Caesar's robe. Why does Shakespeare appear to simplify terms for his audience, especially those who know little about ancient Rome?

43. Contrast examples of errors in judgment, for example, confusion about which side wins the battle and Brutus' opinion of Mark Antony. Why does Shakespeare show the dangers of human frailty? Hasty judgment? Prejudice? Over-confidence? Arrogance?

44. What hints enhance dramatic tension, for example, Popilius Lena's remark about the day's enterprise, Artemidorus' naming of the conspirators, and Octavius' refusal to take direction from Mark Antony? Why does Shakespeare indicate that Messala knows about Portia's death?

45. How does a bad conscience enable Brutus? How would the character change if he felt like a hero or Roman savior? Why does he seem well matched with Portia?

Notes

Notes

Notes

Notes

Notes

Notes

No more "Double, double, toil and trouble…"

You can learn Shakespeare on the Double!™

   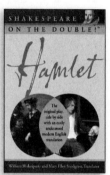

Shakespeare on the Double!™ books make understanding the Bard as easy and painless as this one does. The most comprehensive guides available, they include an easy-to-understand translation alongside the original text, *plus*:

- A brief synopsis of the basic plot and action that provides a broad understanding of the play
- A character list with an in-depth description of the characteristics, motivations, and actions of each major player
- A visual character map that identifies the major characters and how they relate to one another
- A cycle-of-death graphic that pinpoints the sequence of deaths in the play, including who dies, how they die, and why
- Reflective questions that help you identify and delve deeper into the themes and meanings of the play

All *Shakespeare on the Double!* Books
$8.99 US/$10.99 CAN/£5.99 UK • 5¹/₂ x 8¹/₂ • 192–264 pages

The next time you delve into the Bard's masterpieces, get help—on the double!

Available wherever books are sold.

Wiley and the Wiley logo, and Shakespeare on the Double! are trademarks or registered trademarks of John Wiley & Sons, Inc. and/or its affiliates in the United States and other countries.